Looking for Love in Later Life

A Woman's Guide to Finding Joy and Romantic Fulfillment

Monica Morris

Avery Publishing Group

Garden City Park, New York

Cover Photo: Stock Imagery
Cover design: William Gonzalez
Typesetter: William Gonzalez
In-house editor: Linda Stern

Avery Publishing Group
120 Old Broadway
Garden City Park, NY 11040
1-800-548-5757

Library of Congress Cataloging-in-Publication Data

Morris, Monica B.
    Looking for love in later life: a woman's guide to finding joy
and romantic fulfillment / Monica Morris.
        p. cm.
    Includes index.
    ISBN 0-89529-814-7
    1. Dating (Social customs) 2. Mate selection. 3. Middle aged
women. 4. Aged women. 5. Divorced women. 6. Widows. I. Title.
HQ801.M78 1997
646.7'7—dc21   97-19781
                                            CIP

Printed in the United States of America

10   9   8   7   6   5   4   3   2   1

Contents

Acknowledgments

To my publisher, Rudy Shur, heartfelt thanks for your encouragement, your advice, and your enthusiasm for this book from the very first day we spoke of it.

Thank you, too, to my editors, Joanne Abrams and Linda Stern, whose sensible suggestions and thoughtful insights were invaluable.

I also want to express my appreciation to the hundreds of men and women who so generously shared their stories with me and from whom I learned so much, and to colleagues, friends, and family for their continued support and interest in this project.

Finally, this book is dedicated to Clark. He knows why.

Preface

Wanting love in our lives is perfectly natural at any age. It isn't something to be ashamed of, or to deny. It doesn't mean we are needy or dependent or weak. It means, simply, that we are human. Human beings thrive on love. Admitting that we want love is the first step to finding it.

If you've picked up this book, then its title speaks to you; it's meant for you. Keep reading—and if you allow yourself to follow just a few of the suggestions and ideas you'll find here, if you arm yourself with some of the tools, then at the very least your life will be enriched; it may be transformed!

Who am I to suggest how you might look for love? As a sociologist, I've spent many years teaching and writing about social relationships. Far more important, though, has been my experience as a widow, a woman just like you, looking for love in later life.

The tools this book offers you, "a woman who wasn't born yesterday," widowed or divorced or never married, are shaped directly from my adventures—and the adventures of hundreds of single men and women in their fifties and sixties and seventies that I interviewed and who were generous in sharing their stories. I learned a lot—but then I had a lot to learn.

My mother certainly never taught me much about men. Her experience was limited to just one man, my father; she was sixteen when she met him. Her most compelling lesson, and I learned it well, was that I was to be a "good girl" because no decent man would want "damaged goods."

Following my mother's lead, I married an endearing young fellow I met when I was eighteen and gladly hung up my dating-game hat, already fed up with pretending an interest in combustion engines and silly sports, and of struggling to hang on to my virtue!

We planned to live happily ever after, until death did us part, and we did. Then, after forty good years, I was on my own for the first time in my life—and doing what I'd never expected to do again: dating.

It was so strange to be single, especially in a city like Los Angeles, threads of nuttiness woven into its fabric, diverse communities scattered across a hundred miles. My dear friends, adult children, caring colleagues, all helped ease that terrible transition from wife to widow. Finally, though, I was on my own, too busy to be lonely, but aching for the taken-for-granted sharing of everyday events, the ordinary routines, the talking. Most of all, I missed the talking.

Nevertheless, the idea of meeting someone didn't enter my head. I had been teaching in life-cycle courses that for every widower over fifty, there are at least five widows. Over and over again I'd heard that old cliché about all the good men being either married or gay. I'd had a fine, long-lasting partnership with a sweet and loving man. That part of my life was over. Or so I thought.

Some months into my widowhood, a colleague who had passed me in the halls for over a decade with no more than a nod and a "Good morning" invited me to lunch. In turn, I boldly asked him to a concert a couple of weeks later. He turned up at my house wearing his long-dead father's long-out-of-fashion dark suit, not having one of his own and wanting to dress appropriately. This being Los Angeles, appropriate dress for the symphony can be anything from tuxedo to cut-off jeans! Still, his effort was touching and appreciated, as was being driven to the concert hall and delivered safely home.

Once home, what was I supposed to do when he followed me up the steps and into the house? I had no idea.

Fortunately, my colleague was a gentleman, and his interest in me was probably more compassionate than passionate. Whatever his motive, his concern for me helped at that difficult time. To have an attentive friend, yes, a man, call for me, take me out, and bring me home—a date, yet not really a date—was wonderfully life-affirming. It helped me move from the state of being "much married" to that of being a *single woman* rather than a widow, a title I had already accepted as mine for the rest of my life.

My colleague was to be the first of dozens and dozens of dates. Given the statistics, how could that be? Widowers are scarce, and women outnumber men at every age after high school and college. I discovered, though, that the recent trend to later-life divorce brings a large addition to the pool of single men seeking female companionship and often marriage. If I, a sociologist, hadn't known this, surely other women needed the good news too. So I decided to write this book.

For the purposes of "science," I found myself doing things I might never have done otherwise. In a little over a year, I met more than a hundred men, one or two vile and disgusting ones, but most of them pleasant and personable. I've made more good friends than I can count, and I have even been honored with some serious marriage proposals.

What, I wanted to know, are the best ways to find and meet potential partners for people long out of school or college, per-haps even retired from the workplace—those places where young people traditionally find romance? What are the expec-tations between couples these days? I was happily married when men and women became "sexually liberated" so the con-cept had had no significance for me at that time. Now, it was ter-rifying! How was I, rather shy outside the lecture hall and decidedly naive in these matters, to meet men? How was I, who had been one of a couple all my adult life, to venture out as a single? What was the first step?

That first step, and all the steps that followed, I learned the hard way, by trial and error. I discovered at first hand, as well as from hundreds of other mature men and women, what works and what doesn't work in setting out to meet members of the opposite sex. What you will find in the following pages is the result of all that: a straightforward, nuts-and-bolts guide to looking for love in a changed and changing world. The tools you will find here, the dos and the don'ts, the gentle encouragement will help you develop the confident attitude you need to venture into the previously unknown. The resources provided here—where the men are and how to meet them as well as ways to enrich life and make the most of each day—have been tried and tested and rated! I wish I'd had this book in my hand when I started out!

Wearing my researcher's hat was a neat trick! It gave me license to explore the new and mysterious world of relationships far more daringly than perhaps I might otherwise have done. It was almost all enjoyable! And even what was not fun was often funny—at least in hindsight! Along the way, I also learned that I can still fall in—and out—of love. Finally, I'm not quite so naive about sex as I was!

My mother might not want to know that! You, though, reading this book, should have no such qualms! Read on!

It's Not Too Late to Look for Love

I 'm willing to bet that you never thought of yourself as a pioneer! But you are. You—and I—are walking where not many have walked before. The wonderful news is that we are living longer, in better health, than any people in the history of the world! We should be celebrating that, and many of us are. But along with the improvements that bring us ten, twenty, thirty extra years of life have come some changes in the ways we live, changes we didn't bargain for.

Not so long ago, a woman in her fifties or sixties who had lost her husband—and she was usually widowed rather than divorced—was thought of as an old lady whose life was nearly over. That was the way she saw herself too. She stayed home and knitted sweaters for her grandchildren and took care of others for the rest of her life.

You, though, in your fifties, sixties, and seventies, aren't old. You have years and years ahead of you, and there aren't any blueprints for how to spend them. The challenge is to take those added years, that gift, and fill them with life and love—as well as with knitting, if that's what you enjoy. It's a challenge because you know you have to make it happen and you aren't sure where to begin. You are shy about venturing out, afraid of what you might find. You may feel a bit foolish admitting, even to yourself, that you would like to be fulfilling yourself in some way, or that you might enjoy the company of a nice man. It may have been a long time since you were single, and you are unsure of yourself.

Well, take heart! Help is right here. In these pages you'll find encouragement to cheer you on. You'll find tools to help you develop the confidence in yourself and the courage you need to be a pioneer. "Life shrinks or expands in proportion to one's courage," wrote Anaïs Nin. So, be brave!

The confidence to be brave comes with:

§ Having reasonable expectations.

§ Understanding yourself.

§ Getting involved in the world.

§ Preparing for your new life.

§ Knowing you have done your best to look good.

§ Learning how to put your best foot forward.

§ Knowing that what you want is normal.

§ Knowing you can look after yourself.

WHAT ARE YOUR EXPECTATIONS?

At a conversation group I attended, one of the questions put to me was: "If you could choose among all the film stars or entertainers in the world, who would you pick as your type? What kind of man turns you on?"

After a few seconds of thought, I realized that I don't favor any particular type and that my fantasies about a mate have little to do with a man's face or form.

The group persisted. "But what would the man of your dreams be like? Not only his appearance—what qualities would you want?"

They wanted me to give them some ideal—and an ideal is not, and never can be, real. To satisfy the others, though, I managed to list a few necessary characteristics. He would have a good sense of humor, be intelligent, be kind, be in reasonably good physical shape, have a political outlook similar to mine, be able to make good conversation, care about music . . .

One problem for people at any age is this notion of the ideal partner who will look like a film star, meet all our intellectual needs, satisfy our passions—and take out the garbage, as well! That perfect person is out there, somewhere, and we will recognize him at first glance. Electricity will crackle between us. Our eyes will meet and we will both know that we have met our fate.

If only it were so!

Chemistry Is Not the Same as Love

Chances are that the fiercely strong connection you might feel at first meeting with a member of the opposite sex will hold only for a while. You may be drawn together by an overwhelming and irresistible desire that quickly pulls you into each other's arms—perhaps into bed. You won't be able to keep your hands off each other. Sound familiar? It happened to you when you were in high school. It could, and often does, happen between people in their mature years too. The chemistry between you can be so compelling that those desirable characteristics you listed for your ideal mate fly out the window. So what if his politics are to the right of Attila the Hun and you are a socialist? So what if his idea of an enjoyable evening is listening to the music of the pre-Baroque and you are crazy about Loretta Lynn?

You are temporarily insane! At best, and it happens for some people, the fire will cool a little and you will be able to judge each other's suitability more sensibly, learn you do have a lot in common, find you like each other, and decide you can build a firm foundation to a lasting partnership. Just as likely, perhaps far more likely, the flames will soon consume themselves and you will wonder what you ever saw in each other. He's rude to waiters, he's vain beyond belief, he's never on time, he's frugal to the point of meanness, and so on.

The myth of love at first sight sometimes causes a turning away from someone who might, in time, prove a suitable match. A well-known matchmaker told me she had negotiated successful marriages between people who *hated* each other at first sight and wanted never to see each other again. Based on her examination of their tastes, their likes and dislikes, their spiritual beliefs, and the values they each held dear, she knew they were well suited, even if they didn't know it themselves, she said. She insisted that the couple persist in getting to know each other; she wouldn't allow them to give up too soon.

Examine Your Attitudes

If you're looking for romance, whether you are widowed or divorced, it helps to be realistic about what you will find. A problem with widows, so I am told by the men who would like to be romantically interested in them, is their tendency to sanctify their lost husbands, to erase the husband's flaws from memory, and to remember only their husband's better, sweeter, or more generous ways. And then to hold in their minds this polished and perfect creature as the standard by which to judge any new man who might come into their lives. It's a hard act for any man to follow.

For a woman divorced after many years of service to her husband and family, especially if her husband has left her for another woman, often a younger woman, the sense of loss and grief is also real and painful, but may express itself in bitterness, in seeing men as users and takers to be viewed with suspicion.

If you hold any of these images of "the men out there"—as being as handsome as film stars, as never able to measure up to what has been lost, or as bound to be wolves or dirty dogs—you are surely handicapping yourself in the search for another man with whom to share your life.

Women are also pretty hard on *themselves* and see themselves negatively compared with the way men perceive themselves.

A classroom exercise used in training sessions for professionals shows how easygoing men are about their appearance

compared with women. Class members are given a set of statements, the object being to find someone in the group—and the
age range may be from twenty-five to sixty-five—to answer
"true" to each of the statements, including "I feel good about
my body." An instructor for the course tells me that in the
many times he has taught it, hardly ever has he come across a
woman who agrees that she feels good about her body; women
have all kinds of reservations, even if they work out, lift
weights, and look perfect to everyone else. To be sure of finding people with a glowing self-image, the instructor will have
to turn to the men; they'll almost always admit to feeling good
about their bodies. A man tends to see himself as youthful, vir-
ile, and sexy, just as he was years ago, even if no one else sees
him that way.

Comics in newspapers reflect what is going on in the society;
the sudden burst of recognition in an insightful cartoon makes
us smile. In a newspaper cartoon by Gail Machlis headed "Blind
Date," a man and a woman are talking on the telephone. She
asks, "So, how will I know you?" He answers, "Well, I'm tall,
about 6'2", and I used to have red hair." Another, by Wise and
Aldrich, captioned "Personals," shows a newspaper column
with an advertisement reading: "SM [single male]—Slightly
balding, wears glasses, but only for reading, enjoys lawn mow-
ing, walks to get the paper, napping, just sitting around.
Interested? Write Box 402."

Let's face it. Most of us—men and women—are pretty ordinary. Mr. Ideal, by definition, doesn't exist. That doesn't mean you
should accept just anyone, but if you are to be successful in finding a romantic companion, you should have realistic expectations
of him and have a candid—not negative—picture of yourself.

In my early ventures into the dating scene, I soon learned
how inflated were the descriptions that men gave of themselves
in their advertisements and letters, and on the telephone.
Besides overstating their looks, especially their height, they
often understated their age. I was amused that one man advertised himself as "young widower, 58," thinking you would have
to be ninety to consider fifty-eight as young. (It was Colette, I
believe, the French author of *Chéri*, who yearned to be fifty-five

again!") After our first, pleasant meeting, "young widower, 58" confessed he was, in fact, sixty-one (and had been a widower for more than ten years).

"Why would you fib about so *few* years?" I asked.

"I think sixty is the dividing line," he told me. "To say `sixty' in an advertisement is the kiss of death. No one will respond."

That was his belief, but it is far from true. Men who advertise their age as over sixty, or even over seventy, receive many responses, as do women who request a companion of "60-plus" or "60 to 70" or "65 to 75." Even if the women don't include their own age, the implication, at least, is that they, too, are in these age groups.

Don't Let the Statistics Frighten You

It is well known that single women over fifty, whether they are widowed, are divorced, or were never married, outnumber single men of that age. Women, in fact, outnumber men in all age groups after the college years, and the gap increases with age. Statistics, though, can be misleading. If a woman takes them too seriously, they can—and do—stop her from even trying to find a partner in her later years because she feels her chances are small to none.

It helps to know how to interpret the figures. For example, a statistic that lumps all the over-fifties together includes people in their eighties and nineties and even those over one hundred years old! Women are more likely to live to very great ages than are men, and when the figures for very old women are averaged in with figures for the fifties and sixties, the odds can be ten to one or even higher, especially in some residential areas. For instance, many more single women than single men are found in retirement communities like the Leisure Worlds and Sun Cities. In a singles club in one such community, the women are referred to as the "casserole brigade," these women using their cooking skills to woo new widowers! In spite of the occasional matches that are made in retirement communities, if a woman really wants to find a new partner, she should perhaps consider living in a less age-segregated place.

If we waited for new widowers, the odds would be truly formidable. Women are far more likely to outlive their husbands than are husbands to outlive their wives; some women outlive two or three husbands! There are now five widows to every widower in the United States, and widowers have higher death rates than married men in the same age groups. But in this modern world, there are some modern trends, and one is the later-in-life divorce. Most of the fifty-plus single men are divorced, not widowed. Of the one hundred or so men I have met and "dated" in researching this book, only three or four were widowers and only two had never been married. Both of these never-married men had had long-term relationships that had ended either in the death of the woman or in a divorce-like parting.

The trend to later-life divorce brings a new pool of men—and women too—into the dating scene. Newly divorced men may relish their freedom, and some are decidedly giddy at first; but after a year or two many begin to feel the need for a steady or permanent relationship with a woman close to their own age. In their book *Our Turn*, Christopher L. Hayes, Deborah Anderson, and Melinda Blau discuss research into later-life divorce that indicates that for many of the women, however, remarriage is not what they want. In one study, close to half of the sample of 352 divorced women aged forty to seventy-five, who had been in marriages lasting from ten to forty-eight years, did not wish to remarry. Although they missed someone to share their lives with, they loved being independent. While it may not be possible to generalize, this study does seem to indicate that not all women included in those "five or ten women to one man" statistics are, or will be, looking for remarriage.

GET INVOLVED IN THE WORLD!

Even if we were on a level playing field and the numbers of older single men and women were equal, they would never meet each other if they stayed home and watched television. Meeting members of the opposite sex means being actively involved in the world rather than passively waiting. Perhaps your friends will introduce you to someone nice? It does happen—but don't hold your breath!

We know that good jobs don't fall in our laps, either; we have to be out there, hunting. And we don't expand our minds without making some real effort to get into something that stirs our imagination. One way to do that is to join groups and organizations and take classes that sound like fun—and not *only* because you might meet someone at a seminar or on a hike, though that certainly can and does happen. One of my women friends took up square dancing after her divorce when she was fifty-six, in an effort to get in shape and have fun while doing it. She married a fellow do-si-doer within twelve months. Another friend, divorced at fifty-seven after a marriage of thirty-seven years, married a man she met overseas during a two-year stint with the Peace Corps.

It's wonderful if it happens. However, the real motivation for getting out into the world is to keep yourself open to new experiences so you can continue to grow, intellectually and artistically. Still, it doesn't hurt to have lively and interesting stuff to talk about when you do meet a man you'd like to know better.

Get out and do things! That's easier to say than to do, as I well know. When years of social events have been shared with a partner, it is devilishly difficult to venture out on your own, especially if you are shy, especially if you feel unprepared and, perhaps, ungainly and unglamorous. It takes courage and spirit, especially at first. And you won't necessarily enjoy everything you try.

I'll never forget my first temple dance for fifty-plus singles. Since I still smart at the memories of dances I went to in my teens and the agony of standing at the edge of the dance floor *longing* for someone to ask me for a quickstep or a fox-trot, why would I inflict this on myself again? For research, that's why. It was just like being sixteen again except now I prayed I *wouldn't* be asked to dance. The men all seemed like my grandpa—at least a generation older than me—although they *were* energetic dancers.

I did dance, however, much more than when I was in my teens! The band was good, and being whirled around the floor to the jitterbug tunes of the 1940s was quite exhilarating. Few men of fifty-plus here; most were seventy-plus or even eighty-plus; the women generally were a lot younger.

Ballroom dancing isn't really my cup of tea, and I left the dance hours before it was over. Still, I *had* taken the first step into the new and as yet unknown singles world. I had gone out on my own, I had spoken to strangers, I had been invited onto the floor—and I had learned I was free to leave if I wanted to! You don't have to do anything you don't want to do, but do be open to experiences outside your own four walls!

PREPARE YOURSELF FOR YOUR NEW LIFE

You've decided that you'd rather not spend the rest of your life without the company of someone of the opposite sex, whether just for the occasional date or for the long term, and you are willing to get out into the world and have some new experiences to see what you can find.

Are you ready? Or were you so comfortable in your marriage that you feel you let yourself go and now you regret it? Do you feel that no man would find you desirable, that all the other women "out there" are younger, better looking, more self-assured, thinner, and so on, than you are? So, how are you going to prepare yourself?

Think back to when you began dating as a youngster. For many of us those memories have faded, but try to remind yourself of the kinds of preparations you made to go to a movie or for a soda with someone you thought cute or handsome or just nice.

At that time, you were experimenting with your looks: using face packs; steaming your pores open and closing them up again; trying different colognes and perfumes. As a girl, you spent hours styling your hair and putting on your makeup before a date, and you endlessly applied creams and lotions for acne and other skin blemishes. All of this was typical adolescent behavior.

You tried on all the clothes in your closet, agonizing over which was the most flattering thing to wear, which color would best bring out your eyes (and his!), which dress would hide your puppy fat or make more of your nonexistent bosom—and draw attention away from the new pimple on your chin!

In the flash of an eye, or so it seems now, you were married, you reared a family, you saw the children out of the house, and you lost a husband. And in all that time, only rarely did you spend as much time preparing for an outing as you did when you were single.

Couples who have been together for a long time hardly even notice what their spouses look like anymore. It certainly can be maddening when a husband doesn't recognize and comment on a new dress his wife is wearing. But this taken-for-granted attitude in a long-lasting marriage is less a symptom of familiarity breeding contempt than a sign that the pair have so much shared history, so much in common, have grown together in such a way, that each sees the essence of the other rather than the surface, the decoration.

Of course, we do pay some attention to our appearance, especially if we work among the public. Some of us have our hair styled regularly—preferably wash-and-wear cuts that require the least possible time and trouble—and we try to keep our fingernails neat and polished; but in a secure partnership, the intense interest we used to have in every pore of our skin and every hair on our head is replaced with other, more pressing matters.

Well, here you are, single again and in some ways adolescent again, feeling the same old doubts and insecurities about your attractiveness and desirability that you felt in your teens. And you may find yourself, again, taking hours preparing for a date. Men, of course, are also concerned about the impression they make when they are meeting someone. I can't tell you how touched I was when I happened to see the nice man of about seventy, who has since become one of my dearest friends and confidantes, carefully combing his hair as he came to fetch me for our first real date. Just like a teenager taking out a new girlfriend.

Your Age Is Not a Problem

In present day America, far too much emphasis is placed on youthful beauty as the ideal for which we must all strive. Those of us whose teens, twenties, thirties, and forties were long ago are still prodded by advertisers, the media and, increasingly, cosmetic and laser surgeons to push back the years. Women, and men too, spend millions of dollars each year in efforts, usually futile, to look ten or fifteen years younger than they are and to weigh fifteen pounds less than their bones can ideally carry.

We strive for baby-soft skin that only babies can have, and we try to wipe away all the natural signs of aging, including the lovely laughter lines that give testimony to a lifetime of smiling, of a character rich in caring, nurturing qualities.

This is not a battle cry to let ourselves go and plunge into bent and wizened decrepitude! Most of us are going to live long lives. Medical researchers now estimate that if a woman has reached sixty without major medical conditions, she will probably live another thirty years. So, it is essential that we take care of ourselves, do some exercise, eat plenty of veggies, be as attractive as is realistic—and plan to enrich those added years for ourselves and for those around us.

No one would deny that looks are important when meeting new people, but be comforted in knowing that men and women are drawn to each other for all kinds of reasons. Among the people I interviewed was "Emily," a widow of seventy-one. (Quotation marks indicate that the real names have been changed.) Her husband had died two years before I met her, after an illness lasting nearly a decade. In his final years, he was confined to a wheelchair, unable to walk or to do anything for himself. He spent most of his days sitting in front of the television, deeply depressed.

Emily, too, suffered all kinds of ill health. She had severe arthritis and had a hip and two knees surgically replaced not long before our meeting. I walked slowly by her side as she limped painfully to a restaurant near her house where we had dinner. Hardly anyone would have seen her as attractive in any conventional way. Nevertheless, she then had, and still has, an attentive, active, loving man in her life. She met him at a political rally, a fund-raiser for a congressional candidate. He adores her and would like to marry her. She says "No way!" For the time being, at least, she is savoring her release from the physical caring for another and is enjoying the courtship and companionship of her "wonderfully tender lover."

You Don't Have to Be a "Ten"

You may think you have to look like Lauren Bacall, or Linda Dano of *Another World*, if you are to have the fulfilling friendship and love of a member of the opposite sex. It is worth noting, moreover, that dazzling celebrities do not necessarily look so dazzling before the makeup artists have done their work. On a book promotional tour once, I was interviewed twice by a talk-show hostess, first for her national television broadcast and then, a few days later, for her radio show. I hardly recognized her as the same woman on the second occasion. On television, her skin appeared like flawless porcelain, her hair was a masterpiece of design; she was drop-dead gorgeous! She arrived for the radio broadcast in what appeared to be her husband's old raincoat, wearing scarcely a dab of blusher or lipstick, and with her hair scraped back into a rubber band. No one would have given her a second look. I'm willing to wager that the "beautiful people" aren't much more beautiful at home than the rest of us are!

In my experience, and that of men and women I have interviewed, grown-up people are looking more for compatible company than for glamour—although, let's face it, glamour has its points! And you, venturing into or re-entering the dating world, will be more successful if besides being concerned with appearance, you have something captivating to talk about, are doing something in the world, and can speak about what you are doing in an entertaining or lively way. It helps to pay attention to the other person's stories too!

BECOME AN INTERESTING PERSON— AND A PERSON OF INTERESTS

The most boring men and women I have met in the course of collecting material for this book either were retired and doing nothing but watching daytime television talk shows and videos or were still working—and doing nothing but watching television talk shows and videos in the evenings. Why would any man want to spend his time with a woman like that, even though he may understand her condition and may have walked that path himself?

It isn't easy to get back into life after losing a husband to death or divorce. To cook, clean house, remember to change the bed linen, get up and go to the office or store or factory, even to gas up the car, requires more energy than we can seem to find. "What's the point of it?" we might ask, even as those chores give some shape to the days. The very thought of going alone to the movies or the theater or out for a meal makes us shudder. Better stay home. Good friends and caring sons and daughters are a blessing at this time, but they have their own lives to live and other commitments; we know we can't depend on their compassion forever.

Even worse, losses can be piled upon losses. You have your own stories to tell; I have mine. I went back to the university only a week or so after Manning, my husband, died, and my days were filled, as they had always been filled, with preparing and presenting lectures, talking to students in my office hours, meeting with colleagues, and all the other familiar routines. Domestic responsibilities doubled because Manning and I had always shared the chores and now I had more to do than hours to do it in. Such a busy life left little time for thinking about myself, for mourning, for loneliness.

Then, after about a year and a half, the university offered an early retirement package so attractive it would have been foolish to refuse it. I was eligible for it by a fluke and, knowing my job might disappear at any time and I could lose all the benefits of this special retirement offer, I accepted.

Fine! I was walking on air—for about five minutes. Then, I began to grieve. I mourned for my job, and I grieved for Manning as I had not allowed myself to grieve before. All I could see before me was an enormous void. Everything I loved and that gave meaning to my life was gone.

Ultimately, we have to find a new sense of meaning and fulfillment, make new pleasures and find new happiness. Healing takes time; we've been told that over and over again. But until we are healed, we won't be ready for new companionship; we won't be in the right frame of mind.

Gradually, almost against my will, I pushed myself back into the world of work and service, and satisfaction. I found I was qualified to teach home-bound, handicapped children, a new kind of teaching for me. At the same time, I began volunteering at the local chapter of the American Red Cross. There, besides finding ways to use my research and writing skills, I was encouraged—urged—to become a contract teacher for the organization and was soon so involved with all these activities, I had no time to think about "poor me," at least during the day.

Before very long, I found I couldn't do so many things at once; I had to choose. Working with orthopedically handicapped children can be very satisfying. A teacher who takes on just one child at a time sees remarkable progress, but I found it a little isolating compared with the workplace teaching I was doing for the Red Cross. Although not many people would believe it, I'm really rather shy, and talking to a room full of people is one of the few ways I can express my otherwise hidden, "hammy" side. It's such a high to get a crowd of people to laugh!

Eventually, I did workplace teaching a couple of days a week and gave one day a week to International Services, a program of the American Red Cross that traces people who have been separated from their families because of war or civil unrest. I also took course after course offered by the Red Cross for its instructors and for the community. I continued to learn, to meet dozens of people every week, to feel I was doing something useful, and to build a fund of fascinating stories, both funny and dramatic, for the entertainment of my friends and family.

You will find your own new interests, perhaps building on your work experience as I did, perhaps trying work or leisure activities completely different from anything you've done before. A lot will depend on whether you need to work, part-time or full-time, to pay the rent or you have enough coming in from pensions and other assets to be retired from the paid workforce. Try on different activities for size until you find just what suits you.

Even if you are financially secure, you may feel you should be paid for your work. Since the early days of women's liberation, a lively debate has centered around the idea that women have for too long given their time and energy to others who have benefitted from this free labor. You will come to your own conclusions about this idea, based on your own views and circumstances and on the availability, or lack, of paid work where you live. Volunteering your time to a cause you believe in can make you feel wonderfully purposeful and generous, which is no small reward when you are weighing costs and benefits.

Becoming involved, or remaining involved, in your community, whether with a helping agency like the American Red Cross or a free clinic or with the local orchestra or theater group that is operating on a shoestring, will get you out of the house and into another group of like-minded people. You'll be astonished when you see just how many organizations you can choose from: artistic, political, charitable, religious, educational. And you will be welcomed and cherished as a volunteer. Get into something you enjoy, and regard that activity as separate from your search for a new partner. Look at it as mind-broadening and emotionally fulfilling, as giving you an absorbing interest for its own sake, as giving you something to think about and talk about—and there's nothing to stop you from keeping your eyes open, just in case a suitable man happens by!

WHAT YOU WANT IS NORMAL

Wanting companionship and affection—wanting to care for and *be* cared for by someone of the opposite sex—is normal. It is understandable if you have had a happy marriage for most of your life, understandable if your marriage turned out to be disappointing, understandable if you have never been married.

If you are a widow, don't let yourself feel disloyal or unfaithful to your late husband for having these feelings, even if some person unwittingly, or wittingly, pushes your buttons.

There's always someone ready to tell you how you should live your life! About nine months after my husband died, I took off the wedding ring I had worn for forty years and put it in my jewelry box for safekeeping. This was clearly upsetting to an old acquaintance, someone who had known Manning and me for a long time, had watched our progress from our early days as immigrants in the United States.

"How can you *do* that?" she wanted to know. "People will think you didn't love him!"

I felt like screaming at her, protesting my *undying* love, but managed to control myself and maintain my dignity.

"You know that isn't true," I said. "But Manning is no longer here. I am no longer a wife; I am a widow. And very much alive!"

While wanting love and affection is normal, to be *desperate* for love or to *appear* desperate is to open yourself to disappointment, perhaps pity or even ridicule. One of the comedian Milton Berle's nastiest jokes concerns the older woman desperate for a mate. A woman is talking to a man who, it turns out, is newly released from prison after many years behind bars.

"What were you in for?" the woman wants to know.

After he answers that he had been serving time for murdering his wife, the woman is silent for a few moments and then, her voice bright, she says:

"Oh! Then you're *single!*"

A woman who had been widowed for a long time told me about some of her experiences as a single person. She had remarried once, and it had been a disaster, entered into too soon after her widowhood, so eager was she to be a wife again. In addition, she had had several other relationships over the years.

Knowing I was fairly newly single, she was keen to advise me. "If you find a nice man who is interested in you, you shouldn't let him go," she said, "not even if he's old enough to be your father. As long as he's a gentleman, what do years matter? *Any* man is better than no man."

This obvious yearning for a man, *any* man, made me feel sad for her. This kind of desperation, this neediness is likely to turn men away rather than draw them to her. One of my more cynical divorced women friends goes to the other extreme. Quoting the feminist bumper sticker, she jokes, not meaning it at all: "A woman without a man is like a fish without a bicycle!"

If you are to look for and find pleasant male companionship, perhaps love, perhaps marriage, you'll need an attitude that is neither desperate nor disparaging! Stepping out into the world of single people and using the resources all around you require you to have realistic expectations and to keep an open mind. Looking for love calls for courage and some risk-taking.

LOOK AFTER YOURSELF!

Knowing you can take care of yourself, physically and in other ways, is vital if you are to find that needed courage to leave your safe haven and enjoy new experiences. Yes, there are risks to every adventure. In Chapter 6, we'll discuss the kinds of risks you might face and how to protect yourself against them so you can venture out with confidence and self-assurance.

Being a pioneer takes some courage, but preparation is the key to success. So, fasten your seat belt! Here you go!

Chapter Two

Like a Good Girl Scout— Be Prepared!

Y ou're almost tempted to venture out into the unknown. You *would* venture out there, if only . . . If only you were more attractive, sexier, cleverer, funnier, taller, shorter, thinner . . . ? Add any or all adjectives that describe what you see as your shortcomings, including the need to be "younger," and you'll sit at home alone in front of your television set forever.

No one's perfect. You really know that, but for some reason you think you must be perfect to attract a mate or a date. What you *do* need—and I'll come back to this again and again—is confidence.

Confidence is not smugness or brashness or assertiveness. It means feeling comfortable about yourself and knowing you can help other people feel comfortable too. Confidence, or self-assurance, can be developed and strengthened. When someone returns your smile, you feel better about yourself. When someone responds positively to your idea or suggestion, your confidence is reinforced. When your cheerful "Good morning!" is returned, the day becomes sunnier and you feel more closely knitted into the human race.

Making sure you are prepared for new challenges in life is the surest way to build your confidence.

WHAT DO YOU WANT?

Are you looking for a life partner, or would you simply like someone to go to the movies with on Saturday nights—and wake up with on Sunday mornings? Would you like a companion for exotic travel, or are you more interested in hiking in the hills near your home with a pleasant member of the opposite sex? Is the company of a good conversationalist what you would most enjoy? Or would you like someone who can play a musical instrument or sing so you can make lovely music together? Would you prefer to be with someone who just wants to enjoy home life, who will appreciate your good cooking, and who will take an interest in the garden. Or . . .? You may not know exactly what you want until you know who you are. Further, the answer may change with your circumstances, as you may change, as "Janine" and "Frances" changed.

Janine's Story

Janine was widowed after a good marriage of thirty-eight years, and she was sure she wanted to remarry and create a partnership similar to the one she had enjoyed for so long. She had mourned her "George" for over a year and missed the simple routines of her old life. Janine is an excellent homemaker; she loves to cook and always took pride in preparing a fine dinner for George each evening—for which George unfailingly thanked her and complimented her. She looked after the inside of the house, painting and hanging wallpaper; George managed the garden, the cars, and the outside painting. After George died, Janine continued her own chores and, as she'd been left fairly well off financially, she was able to hire tradespeople to do George's work. She firmly believed the ideal match for her would be a man just like George.

In the second year of her widowhood, Janine was offered, first, a consulting job, then a full-time position as an interior decorator. Her home took on different meaning; it became a weekend haven, a place where she could slip into casual clothes and relax—when her brain wasn't still churning over ideas for blending colors and fabrics and shapes to be incorporated into her designs. She continued to cook, sometimes, but found housework took too much of her time and energy, so she hired a housekeeper.

The thought of returning to full-time homemaking, with house and husband as her reason for being, lost its appeal. She loved her new professional self, making her own money, being consulted and respected by her colleagues and clients. Yes, she wanted a man in her life, but he wouldn't be another George.

When she met "Harry," a colleague of one of her clients, he was serving on the board of directors of a major company. He travelled extensively and lived in a full-service luxury apartment that required no maintenance efforts from him. If he owned a screwdriver, he certainly never used it.

The couple married, and a year later Harry retired with as much annual income from investments and stock options as he had previously earned in his job. For the first time in his adult life, he had time on his hands. To Janine's surprise, and his own, Harry became a handyman, fixing shelves, painting, doing odd jobs around Janine's house that they now shared. He discovered George's tools, found he enjoyed repairing things, and began working with wood.

Eventually, he became a creative cabinetmaker. He now designs and builds handmade accent pieces both for their own home and for Janine's clients. He had long been a knowledgeable wine collector, and now he has developed an interest in cooking, taking a cordon bleu course at a local university and occasionally preparing fine dishes for Janine.

Human beings are dynamic creatures, and what they want may change as their knowledge of themselves and their talents changes.

Frances' story

At fifty-eight, Frances was in a different position from that of Janine when "John," her husband, died suddenly. Financially, life had always been a struggle for the couple. John had insisted that Frances be an at-home wife and mother for their three sons, and Frances had been happy with that arrangement.

She enjoyed being a housewife and took pride in shopping economically, cooking nourishing meals, sewing her own curtains, making her own clothes, and knitting all the family's sweaters. When the boys left home, Frances volunteered some time to the local hospital, working with old people.

The couple had next to nothing in savings, and John carried no life insurance except mortgage coverage. Their fine house was a valuable possession, but the substantial mortgage had always strained their budget.

Even with no monthly mortgage to pay, the taxes, maintenance, and upkeep of the house ate up almost all of Frances' tiny widow's pension. The little nest egg was soon gone, and she would have to go out to work if she was not to lose the family home.

Her last job, more than thirty years before, had been as a secretary. Her skills were rusty; she knew hardly anything about computers or word processing. What's more, she would have to travel to the city if she wanted a decently paying office position; her old car was unreliable and public transportation from her suburb was poor.

Fortunately, she found a job near home as a clerk in the bookstore of a local private trade college, a job she found both tiresome and tiring, simply a means to an end. When she was asked how she liked working in the bookstore, she would answer "I don't want to talk about it; it's boring, boring, boring." To add a little to her wages, she rented her spare room to a woman teacher and was irritated at "having to tiptoe around a stranger."

Except for the joy she found in her two young grandchildren, Frances didn't have much else to comfort her. She longed for her old life; she missed John and the simple pleasures they'd enjoyed together. Looking back on it, she could see that their life had been filled with riches.

Only a few blocks away, in the same neighborhood, "Stan" was still recovering from the death of his wife a year before. He had devotedly nursed her through a long and terrible illness, and felt physically and emotionally drained. His house, built at the same time and by the same builder as Frances' house, was neglected, as was his one-man business. He was lonely and low-spirited, despite the efforts of his two adult daughters and three small grandchildren to cheer him up. He was also short of funds and knew he must soon find a job or start another small business.

When Frances and Stan exchanged glances across the aisle in the local supermarket, they each sensed they had seen the other before. It turned out that Frances and Stan's wife had carpooled, both members of a group of mothers in the neighborhood who, years before, took turns in driving their children to school. Once or twice, Stan had collected Frances' boys when his wife had had other commitments.

Together, Frances and Stan retraced their almost parallel pasts, realizing that their children had known each other and had celebrated birthdays and other events together long ago.

As their acquaintanceship was changing to friendship, then affection, then love, Stan, having no capital to start a new business, took a job in the city—as a temporary measure, he insisted.

Frances, still working at the college, was worried when she learned that the owner of the bookstore was planning to sell. When he did, he warned her, she might lose her job.

"But wouldn't that be the perfect little business for us?" Stan saw the opportunity and went for it. He sold his house to raise capital and moved into Frances' home. The two were now married.

Work at the bookstore took on new meaning for Frances. As an owner, she looked forward to each day's challenges. She and Stan gradually expanded the business, buying other college bookstores for greater efficiency and higher profit. The couple worked well and patiently together.

Frances is now a capable businesswoman; she is no longer bored at work, nor does she have any wish to return home as a full-time housewife. Her wants changed with the circumstances.

The stories about Janine and Frances show us that "What do you want?" may have to be put differently. Perhaps, "What do you want *right now*?" or even "What do you *think* you want?" Neither woman started out wanting to change, and neither could have imagined how her life would be transformed. The way each responded to new situations as they arose indicates the wisdom of remaining flexible in one's thinking, of taking one step at a time, and of seeing and seizing opportunities as they come your way.

WHO ARE YOU?

One of the most important elements of knowing what you want is knowing yourself. "Twenty Questions"—perhaps more properly called "Twenty Answers"—is a popular exercise college instructors often give to their classes. Students are asked to give as many answers as possible—preferably twenty or more—to the question "Who are you?" When I used this exercise with my students, I asked both *"Who* are you?" and *"What* are you?" to bring out as many answers as possible. Still, some people could dredge up no more than four or five answers: "I am female, a student, Catholic, young, unmarried. . . ." I termed these "demographic" answers, the kind you find in census statistics, not having much to do with who the person *really* is.

Accentuate the Positive!

As an exercise, take a piece of paper and see how many qualities you can write down that describe who and what you think you are. After listing the demographics, what other kinds of answers did you scribble? Music lover? Artist? Cook? Nature lover? Intellectual? Bicyclist? Knitter? Athlete? Couch potato? Hiker? Dancer? Butterfly brain? Friend? Typist? Engineer? Sailor? Driver? Sister? Aunt? Go on! There's more. And while you're at it, you might include some of the qualities you *could* have if you applied yourself, some of the things you'd *like* to be. Aspiring writer? Would-be poet? Potential computer expert?

When you have finished your list—and you may have thought of a hundred items that describe you or could describe you—arrange the items in order of importance to you. Is music, listening to it or playing it, such a passion that your pleasure in living would be less without it? What kind of music means most to you? If you love the Baroque, could you enjoy the company of someone who finds Bach boring? Or could you be with someone who looks down his nose at jazz if you can't keep your feet still when Benny Goodman swings? Of course, you could get through an evening or two. Could you do so forever? Only you can decide what compromises you would, or would not, make for the person who might be attractive and attracted to you.

The ordering of your list may give you some clues, too, about where you might be looking for a mate. You are not likely to meet your match at a Liberal Party club meeting if you are a staunchly conservative Republican—although one can never be sure of even that. It's always a good idea to keep your options open. Ideally, you'll attend events that interest you and stimulate you.

Know Your Strengths and Accomplishments

Many of us women tend to downplay our achievements and our accomplishments and to emphasize our weaknesses, even to ourselves. Perhaps especially to ourselves. If you were blessed, as I was, with doting grandparents who always made you feel you were the cleverest and most beautiful little girl in the world, some of that wonderful sense of being able to do anything you set your mind to has stayed with you. More likely, though, you have only occasionally allowed yourself to feel "superior" in any way.

Now is the time to remind yourself of your good qualities and to dwell on them until you recognize yourself for the valuable, desirable person you are.

Again, take a piece of paper and a pencil and begin writing down all the good things about yourself. What might—and do—other people like about you? How might you make someone else's life better and richer? What can you do well? What *could* you do well if you tried? Include everything good about you, no matter how unimportant it might seem.

§ I bake a wonderful piecrust.

§ I can organize a good party.

§ I'm a good listener.

§ I have elegant handwriting.

- ♪ I can compose a good letter.
- ♪ I manage money well.
- ♪ I have a good sense of humor.
- ♪ I have pretty legs.
- ♪ I'm a good dancer.
- ♪ I can fix a leaky tap.
- ♪ I play a good game of golf.
- ♪ I'm good at my job.
- ♪ I know a lot about. . . .

Keep going and you'll realize just how much you "bring to the table"—much more than you thought.

Yes, you also have a less attractive side. We all do. And, yes, you can change some things: You need not be so grudging in your praise of others, if that's one of your not-so-nice traits. *Tell* someone she looks good in that outfit, or that you appreciate what she's doing, or that her new hairstyle suits her, rather than keeping those compliments bottled up inside you. On the other hand, you can hold your tongue instead of blurting out that less-than-kind remark. But don't waste your time fretting about something hurtful you may have said, or something positive you left unsaid, long ago. Think about *now*! Think positive! Take that list of "the best of you" and pin it on the wall and look at it every day!

ARE YOU EMOTIONALLY READY?

If you are still hurting deeply from the loss of a beloved husband or the ending of a love affair, wait a while. Mourning takes time. "But I'll always grieve for my husband," I can hear you say. "He was my life. I'll never forget him."

"Miriam," a widow who claimed she was serious about remarrying, asked me, "How do you think a new husband would feel about my keeping a framed picture of `Mort' [her late spouse] on display? I just couldn't bear not to see his face every day."

I suggested, as gently as I could, that when she met the man she cared enough about to marry, she might be ready to put Mort's picture away. Perhaps it was too soon to think about a new commitment.

Your good marriage of long duration can't simply be forgotten, neither can nor should the memory of a wonderful partner be put aside. Those shared years of joys and struggles, of rearing children, of successes, and of disappointments too are part of you, part of what you've become. No new partner who cares about you would expect you to abandon the past or ever to forget the person who was the center of your life. But he is entitled to be central to your new and future life together. If this expectation makes you feel disloyal, you are probably not yet ready for a new marriage or partnership.

Joanna's Story

"Joanna," widowed just over a year, was ardently courted by "Alvin," a man with whom she felt she had a great deal in common. Alvin's political and religious beliefs matched hers. He was a writer as well as a jazz critic, although he didn't play an instrument. Joanna's late husband, "Daniel," had also known a lot about music and had fronted his own band as a semiprofessional musician.

Alvin invited her to a jazz festival out of town. This was to be their first time away together, the first time Joanna had shared a bedroom with any man other than Daniel. She regarded it as something of a test, she told me. Alvin was head over heels in love with her and wanted to marry her as soon as she would name the day; Joanna liked Alvin and enjoyed his company and his loving attention, but she wasn't sure about the depth of her feelings for him.

After a drive of several hours, the couple arrived in the coastal town, checked into their hotel, and went straight out to the first musical event of the festival, a big band bash.

"The audience sat at round tables and listened to dance music, swing rather than jazz, number after number, hour after hour. Dance music is for *dancing*, in my opinion, but everyone there just *sat*. I found myself getting more and more frustrated, longing to get up and move to the music. Alvin was having a great time, sitting there snapping his fingers and nodding his head, tapping his feet and shouting 'Yeah, man!' like a silly teenager. When the band began playing some of the romantic songs of the fifties, I found tears welling up, and I had to leave the hall to sob by myself in the ladies' room! Those were songs that Daniel sang to me during all our years together; the Sinatra numbers, especially, upset me.

"When I got back to the table, Alvin was still snapping his fingers and nodding and looking really foolish to me. Undignified. I hated myself for being such a pain, such a . . . snob, I suppose, such an ingrate, but I told him I'd like to leave the concert. Would he drive me to our hotel, just a short distance away, and go back and listen to the music on his own? I didn't want to spoil his pleasure, but I couldn't bear to stay a moment longer."

Alvin was very patient and understanding. He did as Joanna asked and returned to their hotel room after midnight, when the concert was over. Joanna heard him come in but pretended to be asleep. She clung to the very edge of the king-sized bed, curled up tightly, her back to Alvin, effectively shutting him out. He, in turn, kept to the other edge of the bed, hardly moving all night and hastily moving his arm or leg back if it inadvertently touched her.

Joanna recognized that she hadn't finished her grief work and that it would be unfair to Alvin, or any other man, to get married again just yet. To use Daniel as a yardstick against which to measure another man was also unfair, especially as her memories of him were selective.

"Didn't *Daniel* ever embarrass you—or himself?" I asked her. She thought about the question for some moments before admitting that, yes, he'd had his faults, of course. "He was a human being with human flaws"—she searched in her purse for a tissue and mopped at her tears—"but I *knew* them and accepted them."

Traditionally, one year is the time allotted for mourning a deceased spouse, but different people grieve differently. Some people push their grief aside, press on with their lives as though nothing had changed, and then are hit with the full realization of their loss two, three, or even five years later. The world of work doesn't allow much time—two or three weeks at most—for a person to "recover" from the death of a partner and get back on the job. We put on a brave face for the sake of people around us, and that may be one of the ways our pain gets pushed into the back of our mind. It doesn't go away.

Widows seem to "know" when they are ready to move on from mourning and to consider looking for a new love in their lives, just as they seem to know when they aren't ready. A dear friend, widowed for three years, is for the first time venturing out on a singles' hike in her community. "It's taken a while, but I know now that 'Doug' [her husband of forty years] would have wanted me to live as full a life as possible. For me, that includes male company. Doug knew that. I used to be such a flirt, but that part of me seemed to die when Doug died. The flirt is coming back. I can feel it!"

Other widows have told me that the memories of times shared with their husbands will always remain, of course, but that they finally can recall those times without sadness. They feel ready to begin creating memories with someone new.

While a deceased husband can become angelic in memory, divorce often leaves a residue of bitterness as well as sadness. Divorced people too and those recovering from a recently ended love affair are wise to wait until their pain has eased before they look for another partner.

Sally's Story

"Sally," divorced for nearly twenty years, told me of her grief at the breakup, some three years before, of a longtime relationship with "Peter." She had mourned him so deeply that she couldn't, wouldn't—until now—consider someone new in her life.

"When my *marriage* finished, I walked away and hardly looked back. The divorce was a long time in the making, and if anything, it was a relief to both of us to have it over. The early days of our marriage had been wonderful, but as the years went by, our anger kept growing. We tried counseling, we both tried to change, but nothing worked.

"After the eight years of living with Pete, though, I went into such a terrible depression, I wanted to die. He was the one I should have married, but he said he wasn't the marrying kind, even though we bought a house together and fixed it up. We were married in every way except legally. Then he simply walked out on me. . . . I was in such a bad way, I was put on Prozac (an antidepressant medication) for a while! Me, a health nut who never puts anything chemical in my system if I can help it!"

Sally's pain when Peter walked out of her life was as severe as if he had died. Eventually, with time—and some professional help—her wounds healed, and she knew she was ready to let go of the past and move on.

FEAR OF PUTTING YOUR FOOT IN IT

Perhaps, though, while you know you are emotionally ready to consider looking for love, you are still afraid of new situations, of saying the wrong thing and making a fool of yourself.

Are you shy? Do you get tongue-tied talking to strangers? Do you look down or away rather than talk with someone you've never met before? Is it difficult for you to meet the eye of someone new, yet when you are among people you know well, you are relaxed and can chat and laugh and enjoy yourself without thinking about the impression you are making?

Shyness is surprisingly common. Even people constantly in the public eye struggle with being shy. Stage fright, an extreme form of shyness, is a problem for many well-known actors and performers. Joseph Lhevinne, an internationally renowned piano virtuoso, was reputedly so nervous before a concert that his wife would literally have to shove him onto the stage. Sir Laurence Olivier, too, suffered a period of such terrible stage fright during a run of *Othello*, he became physically ill before each performance.

People never believe me when I confess that I am shy. For years as a university professor, I stood up in front of classrooms filled with people, lectured, often joked, and appeared unselfconscious and assured. I have also presented dozens of scholarly papers at professional conferences, appeared on television programs, and narrated radio documentaries. The trick is to hide the shyness, and that can be done in several ways.

Know What You're Talking About

The appearance of self-assurance in professional settings comes when a speaker is completely in command of her material. That takes work. Every fact must be checked and rechecked beforehand; all references have to be in hand; alternate theories or points of view are understood and can be addressed and dismissed, if necessary. The successful speaker knows her audience, knows the subject matter, and is ready to defend her position when questioned.

This calls for learning the most effective techniques of speaking, for lots and lots of practice, sometimes with a tape recorder or even a video camera, and for changing or getting rid of awkward quirks or tics.

I'll never forget the time I caught the professor I most admired—and feared—psyching himself up just before he entered the lecture hall. Usually, I was seated in class before he arrived, but this time I was following him down the hall, trying not to let him see me. I was in such awe of him, I knew I would stammer and stumble if he spoke to me.

The professor stopped at the classroom door, straightened his back, and pulled himself up to his full height. Then, to my surprise, he composed his face, putting on a rather stern expression and settling into it for a few seconds before turning the door knob and sailing majestically into the hall, where the students immediately hushed into a respectful silence.

It was only then that I realized that this famous scientist was human and that he quite deliberately put on a mask before facing an audience.

Tricks of the Trade

You don't have to be a professor or a public speaker to use some of the tricks that work for professionals. You can practice before entering any unfamiliar social situation. Ask yourself:

§ What kinds of questions might you ask a stranger?

§ How would you ask those questions so you appear interested rather than just plain nosey?

§ What do you want to know about this person?

§ What questions would be acceptable to him or her?

§ How would you answer if those questions were asked of you?

§ Can you give a gracious answer to a question you think is too personal?

§ What subjects can you talk about with confidence?

§ What interests you or excites you? Music? Politics? Cooking and nutrition? Movies? Gardening? Try to bring those topics into the conversation in a natural way.

§ Listen to yourself on tape. Do you like what you hear? Can you change what you don't like?

If you have done some homework and are sure of yourself and if you are genuinely interested in the person you are speaking to, you will lose your shyness or, at the very least, you will hide it.

MATURITY AS AN ASSET

Before you go any further, please try to put aside all negative thoughts about age. When I became aware that women in their thirties and forties worry that they are too old to meet a mate, too old to be attractive, I realized how common this lack of self-confidence is at almost every stage of life. Sometimes, there seems to be a conspiracy directed at making us feel unsure about ourselves, young and not so young alike. One television entertainer suggests, even promotes, the idea that it's "all over" for women once they turn forty—though she's about forty, herself. Because men of any age are interested only in young chicks, she says, there is nothing to do but join "the old hags club"!

This may be a great gimmick for her program, especially as she looks like no one's idea of a hag, but don't believe a word of it! Remember that Sophie Tucker, the Red Hot Momma herself, taught us that life *begins* at forty. She knew, and current research supports this, that life can get better and better in the years that follow forty.

Those of us in our fifties, sixties, seventies, or even our eighties are making history. Lydia Brontë, in her extensive study of long life and creativity (*The Longevity Factor: The New Reality of Long Careers and How It Can Lead to Richer Lives*), sees a "second middle age" added to our lives. The years between fifty and seventy-five can be extraordinarily rich and creative, she found.

Brontë writes of a number of distinct patterns of creativity among older people. Some retire from lifelong careers and then return to work, but make major changes in their primary interests, taking up writing or art or going into business for themselves. The workplace is no longer as stable as it once was, so Brontë suggests using retirement, especially early retirement, as an opportunity to retool for new careers. Other people, not required to retire, simply continue working productively in their jobs or careers well into their eighties and later.

We are an aging society, and as the baby-boomers, the largest group of people ever to have been born in the same time period in the United States, move through adulthood, being old is becoming sexy! Some of the film stars popularly viewed as heartthrobs are certainly not in their teens or twenties, nor are they necessarily conventionally beautiful or good-looking. Paul Newman, handsome no matter what his age, is in his seventies! Many other leading actors and actresses, such as Jessica Tandy, and Don Ameche for instance, remained box office attractions well into their sixties, seventies, and beyond.

The judges at a recent Ms. Senior America pageant in California expressed astonishment at the elegance, the poise, and the talents of the contestants, whose ages ranged from sixty to seventy-nine. Not only were the women attractive—"Look at her legs!"—they were also active and energetic, experienced and wise, determined to live every day fully, serving their communities in numerous ways, and continuing to learn. Some had taken up music; some had begun new careers; others developed a taste for adventure and travel. One judge said he was impressed by how many of the contestants referred to things they had done in the past five years. They weren't looking back to when they were twenty or thirty. "It's like they've experienced a rebirth."

This "rebirth" is possible for all of us, and it doesn't mean that we *must* be in the workplace, or that we *must* be in "productive" careers, or that we have to be as glamorous as Joan Collins. It does not mean we must be musical or literary or artistic. To be reborn is to look forward, bringing with us wisdom gained from the past. Our experience is a valuable resource, helping us keep a sense of balance, of reality, as we try new activities, meet new people, and live every day as an adventure. We can use those extra twenty or thirty years fully and positively, or we can let them go to waste.

FITNESS AND WELL-BEING

The achievers in Brontë's study of creative older people had high exercise rates. Physical activity appears to benefit both body and mind. For most of us, regular, moderate exercise is enough to maintain a healthy heart and a feeling of well-being. For general fitness, a brisk walk for half an hour to an hour, three or four times a week, is considered adequate by many medical practitioners, although people who have been working out all their lives may feel much more is necessary. Some of my friends do not feel right unless they spend at least an hour each morning building muscles at the gym, followed by a half hour's swim and some brisk jogging in the evening. They suffer guilt if they skip any of this. Ideally, you'll work out an exercise program that feels right for you, that gives you maximum benefits with minimum wear and tear on muscles and ligaments.

The very latest studies show that being physically fit is a powerful force for health. A team led by Steven N. Blair, director of research for the Cooper Institute for Aerobics Research in Dallas, studied 25,341 men and 7,080 women who received physicals at the clinic between 1970 and 1989. The study found (among other things) that being physically fit is such a powerful force for health that even smokers with high blood pressure and high cholesterol who are in good aerobic shape tend to live longer than nonsmoking couch potatoes who are otherwise healthy.

Further, weight-bearing exercise, like brisk walking, slows down loss of bone density and helps prevent osteoporosis, if it is done regularly. It's a good idea to vary your route. Perhaps walk on level ground for half an hour or so on one day and walk up and down hills the next day, just so you don't get bored and give up!

You will make your own decisions about amount and frequency of exercise, as long as you do *some*—and make sure you get a medical checkup before you start any regular exercise program.

Body Weight

At risk of being shot as the messenger who brings the bad news, I am told by several professional matchmakers that the most difficult clients to match are those who are overweight. Individuals who are overweight, if they are accepted as clients, are told they may have to be matched with someone who is also heavy. If you consider yourself seriously overweight and feel that this may be keeping others from making that initial contact, and may also be compromising your health, you might consider a weight-loss program that encourages sensible eating and exercise. As everyone who has tried knows, it is not easy to shake off the extra pounds, and once the weight has been lost, eternal vigilance is needed to keep it off.

Even though, according to recent reports, the majority of Americans—60 to 75 percent, depending which study is cited—weigh more than they should for good health, few people find overweight attractive. Those few *are* out there, I've learned. Some men do prefer heavy women to slender ones although fewer women appear to prefer heavy men. In my research, I have so far interviewed only one man, a widower, who was looking for a *really* heavily built woman, a woman like his late wife whom he had loved deeply. He was disappointed that the chubby women who responded to his newspaper and magazine advertisements, in which he stated his preference clearly, were rarely heavy enough for his taste!

While the search for a truly large woman may be unusual, several men I have spoken with do talk fondly of women who are "shapely," "zaftig," "curvy," "pleasantly plump," and so on, indicating that the current skinny look is of little interest to them. They do not, however, often include "fat" or "obese" as desirable characteristics.

Far more important than how others feel is the way you feel about yourself. Whether you feel that you have just a few pounds to lose or that you are many pounds heavier than the "ideal," don't allow those feelings to stop you from getting out in the world, enjoying new experiences, and looking for love. Stand tall, hold yourself with pride, and never doubt your worth!

Dress and Grooming

"Ann Landers," "Dear Abby," and other advice columns frequently publish letters of complaint from women about the slovenliness of men. A "Crabby Road" cartoon reinforcing this idea suggests that women who think about getting remarried should just throw some men's grubby underwear on the floor . . . and presumably they'll think again! Not only are husbands reported as sloppy about their appearance and their living habits, but so, too, are men who are trying to attract a date or a mate.

Men are getting a bad rap here. They aren't all slobs, even though they are likely to see themselves as devastatingly dashing and debonair when they haven't shaved for three days and are wearing a tank top and shorts to take a lady to lunch. Still, the point is worth making. We women generally think we know what it takes to be attractive to the opposite sex, and our problem is to measure up to our own, often unrealistic, expectations.

Unfortunately, it's not always easy to tell what kind of clothes are appropriate, especially as standards are constantly changing and what was once considered well-dressed may now seem over-dressed. If in doubt, why not simply ask what level of formality is acceptable at a given event? Are pants acceptable? And must they be dressy, or can they be casual?

New clothes can work wonders in lifting our spirits and our self-confidence, but it is important not to get too carried away by the latest fads and fashions. The trick is to choose what suits you best from among the newest styles. Very short skirts look great on women with pretty legs—and the nerve to show them off. However, longer, slim-fitting or gently flared skirts might be more attractive if your knees, like mine, are less than perfect. Tights look good on some women but may be a bit too revealing on others.

Some older women may have more generous tummies than they once did. Slender skirts worn with slightly fuller tops that tip the hips, will draw the eye up, up, and away, especially if there's a colorful scarf or an attractive piece of jewelry at the throat. Some of us used that trick when we were pregnant! It still works.

Very full, floating, or tentlike skirts and tops, rather than concealing, may actually exaggerate a woman's size. A dear friend and colleague recently taped some lectures for television. She was stunned when she viewed the completed video. "I look as though I weigh three hundred pounds!" she complained. While it's true that the camera might have added the appearance of some extra weight, her loose, flowing garments made her look mountainous even though she is shapely and well-proportioned. She now knows she must wear something a little more form-fitting. If you have access to a video camera, it's fun to have someone take pictures of you in the clothes in your wardrobe—and be sure to take a good, brutally honest friend with you when you shop for new outfits!

LOOKING YOUR BEST

What suited you when you were twenty may not do as much for you now. Even the colors that drew attention to your gorgeous brown eyes and enhanced your creamy skin tones then may not work as well now. Nature and chemistry perhaps have changed the color of your hair, and weather and time have altered the texture of your skin.

This has happened gradually. While you have probably made some changes to your makeup over the years, now may be the time for a critical appraisal of your face and hair. You may decide you are perfect as you are—in which case, congratulations! Or you may decide on change so dramatic that your children wouldn't know you if they met you in the street! More likely than either of these choices, you will want to make some changes, but remain recognizably yourself.

Makeup and Hairstyles

Relatively inexpensive ways of gaining an outsider's view of yourself and how your appearance might be improved or brought up to date are the department store beauty salon makeover—frequently offered as a "special"—and the photographic glamour shots "transformation."

Beauty salon makeovers sometimes include hair cutting and styling, as well as liberal use of the makeup the technician will encourage you to purchase. The hour or two of personal attention, sometimes including a facial massage, can be relaxing and comforting in an atmosphere of some luxury, and you shouldn't feel pressured into buying anything you don't want. If the hair stylist is good, you will emerge with a new, elegant coiffure, some suggestions about hair coloring, and probably rather more makeup on your face than you usually wear, especially in the daytime! You may also pick up some good, contemporary makeup tips.

Often, one of the most dramatic changes you can make in your appearance is by restyling your hair and, possibly, by giving it highlights or a completely new color. If you take a look at old movies, you'll see how hair styles change each decade or so. Some of us are stuck in a time warp; we are still wearing our hair as we did in our teens or twenties. That style suited our faces then, perhaps suits our faces *still*, but is hopelessly out of fashion.

Glamour Shots photography sessions are great fun and can provide good information about the most flattering hairstyles, clothes that enhance a person's best features, and makeup both to conceal blemishes and to reveal assets. (Glamour Shots studios can be found in forty-one states, in Canada, and elsewhere. Call 1-800-GLAMOUR for information.) The technicians are trained to make clients feel pampered. You will finally be shown a slew of pictures of yourself with a range of different looks so you can see how your appearance can be changed. You need not purchase pictures— but you will probably want to!

I had a wonderful time at my local Glamour Shots studio! It was not only the hairdo and makeup that changed me so dramatically but also the four different outfits I chose from the racks of colorful dresses and suits and jewelry provided just for the photo shoot. I was amused to find that the garments are split up the back so they'll fit almost anyone. In the course of the photo session I discovered a flamboyant side to my personality I didn't know existed (a fluffy feather boa and a floppy wide-brimmed hat not being my standard garb!) and the man behind the camera flirted with me so outrageously. I was reduced to giggles and eyelash flutterings that were decidedly out of character and made for marvelous pictures!

These makeover photography studios usually offer low-cost specials around high school graduation time and before holidays, and you will probably find the proofs so attractive you may be tempted to buy some finished pictures. I ordered a set of wallet-sized prints to use for professional purposes—and to include when writing to someone whose personal advertisement asked for a picture. In those pictures I'm wearing a white tailored jacket with a stand-up collar and silver buttons—a garment that you won't find in my wardrobe!

I love watching the makeover programs on talk shows! At one time, the psychologist Dr. Joyce Brothers, with her customary good grace, agreed to be updated on the show *Geraldo*. The change in her appearance was astonishing, not only because of her new, becoming hairstyle but also because the stylists exchanged her frumpy, shin-length greenish suit for a bright red, shiny leather one with a mini skirt that exposed her legs almost to the crotch! She sat next to her daughter, who helped ease her mother's embarrassment by draping *her* long, full skirt over both her own and her mother's legs! Dr. Brothers was made marvelously glamorous, but as she said, this look was not for every day!

Cosmetic Surgery

Aesthetic, or cosmetic, surgery is becoming increasingly commonplace and is no longer reserved for film stars and the very rich, although it is certainly costly. Surgical techniques have been developed, and are still being developed, that give more natural and less obvious results than once were the case.

Still, while cosmetic surgery is thought of as minor because no internal organs are involved, it is serious surgery with all the risks that that implies and should be considered soberly, every aspect investigated thoroughly. Television talk shows present enough evidence of botched faces and distorted breasts to give us pause before committing to the scalpel!

Further, if you expect a face-lift to transform your life, you are bound to be disappointed. It will not even transform your face; it will merely make you look, perhaps, more rested or a bit fresher. I've occasionally seen before and after pictures of real people (not models in advertisements) on television programs, and I found it difficult to see much or any real change after the surgery. If you are sixty, a face-lift may make you look the best you can look at sixty. It may even make you look fifty-five or fifty-six, but it will not make you look thirty; and no reputable surgeon will make such a promise.

Some people may consider a facial feature so "ugly" as to have caused them embarrassment all their lives. The drooping "wattle" under the chin, the heavy eyelids—often family traits—or the bulbous nose can make us painfully uncomfortable in this beauty-conscious society; surgery may make a real difference in those cases. "Beth," a woman in her late sixties, happily married for a third time, recently had neck surgery to remove flesh she had hidden with scarves since her teens. She now proudly wears low-necked blouses to display her newly revealed sleekness! Note, though, that she did attract three husbands—even with her fleshy neck—and her current husband constantly assured her that he loved her as she was.

If you are considering cosmetic surgery, please take the time to investigate fully. You have only one face and body. Call your state medical board about any surgeons on your list. Are there malpractice suits against them? Compare surgeons not only for their price but, of far more importance, for their training.

What board certifications does the surgeon hold? More than twenty medical boards offer certification. Some are legitimate; others are self-designated and may not serve your purpose.

Beware of slick advertisements. Take time to interview at least three surgeons. How many procedures do they perform each year? The more they do, the better they usually are.

Some people get hooked on cosmetic surgery, always expecting that the next procedure will so change them that they will land that super job, find the love of their life, or—more sadly—be able to love themselves. Cosmetic surgery can certainly enhance a person's looks; on occasion, it can work miracles. But you will be disappointed if you expect it to put the clock back twenty or thirty years—or even ten years. You will certainly investigate other, much less extreme measures such as a professional makeover and hair styling first!

NOW YOU'RE COOKING!

You have taken some time to assess yourself as objectively as you can. You are looking and feeling a bit better, perhaps a lot better, than you did. That snappy new haircut suits you, or the new tailored outfit minimizes your waistline and encourages you to stand tall. You have a few new things in your wardrobe that flatter your form. That dark blue sweater really brings out the deep blue of your eyes, and you can apply makeup so it completely covers the dark patches on your cheek yet looks absolutely natural!

You've been boning up on your state history—the ordeals of the Donner Pass party perhaps or the battle of Wounded Knee—or you've become interested in the composition of herbal supplements, or you're learning to play bridge. . . .

You are ready to scan the local newspaper for events geared to your interests. That conversation evening program on the other side of town next Thursday seems likely. You call and speak to the moderator. She is welcoming. That mixer for the fifty-plus crowd might be appropriate. The walking tour led by the local historical society looks intriguing.

Yet you still have doubts. You still feel you aren't ready to meet a lover, a spouse, a significant other. You still aren't . . . perfect. You're still not in shape.

Of course you aren't perfect! You never will be, nor will you ever meet anyone else who is perfect. Allow yourself to be human, and when you meet new people, you'll understand that they are human too. Very few of us are without some doubts about our abilities and our attractiveness when we enter new situations. Trying to make others comfortable with themselves will help you forget yourself and what you see as your short-comings. And take another long look at your list of "good" char-acteristics!

Two more things! Greeting any person of the opposite sex as a new acquaintance, rather than as a prospective lover, will help ease the strangeness. Finally: *Courage!*

Chapter Three

Personal Advertisements

In a little over a year I met and dated over one hundred men, nearly all in my preferred age range: mid-fifties to upper-sixties. Most of them were decent, intelligent people—non-smokers, every one! Some were simply looking for a companion to accompany them to the theater, to the movies, or on walks along the beach; others had more permanent relationships in mind and were looking for the right someone to enhance their lives, to share with them more than just an evening of music, or dinner. These latter men included some who had been long married and who declared that marriage was their natural state.

Several of the men I met took more than a fleeting interest in me. I have formed solid friendships with a handful of them—and have felt a bit more than friendship for one or two. (Readers might be interested to know that just as I was putting the finishing touches to the manuscript of this book, I met the dear man with whom I plan to spend the rest of my life!)

The bumper-sticker slogan "So many men, so little time" began to take on personal meaning because far more men were drawn into my "net" than I could possibly meet. I had, after all, a house, a garden, and a car to care for, work responsibilities, deadlines to meet, children to keep in touch with, letters to write to family and friends across the country and abroad, and on and on.

Friends graciously assure me that I'm "quite nice-looking"—whatever that means—but I am not a great beauty; heads do not turn as I walk by. I am over sixty and not getting any younger. The question, then, is how did I do it? Where *are* all those eligible older men?

Let me assure you, they do exist. The task is to find them and meet them. Meet a lot of them until this new situation feels comfortable and you can act naturally and be yourself.

Because this book grew out of my own need to know about today's dating climate, I'll retrace some of my own experiences so you can see how nervous I was and how I was occasionally embarrassed and made to feel foolish. I'll also suggest how you might avoid some of the minor humiliations I endured! You'll see what worked best for me, and what didn't work at all. And I'll offer some options that might suit people with different interests and requirements from mine.

I was horribly naive at first, shy and gauche. I believe I giggled a great deal, which may be charming in one's teens but is not particularly endearing in maturity. Even though I have served in professional capacities for a long time and I am used to meeting people in boardrooms and classrooms, the last time I had dated was over forty years before—and I had found meeting boys uncomfortable and awkward then! This was an entirely different time and place. I had no idea what to expect—and I didn't know the rules.

PERSONAL ADVERTISEMENTS

I have never cared much for spectator sports, but I do love to walk. A friend, to whom I had talked about joining a walking or a hiking group, gave me a copy of *The Southern Sierran*, a publication of the local Sierra Club. Among the personal advertisements, I found this:

Handsome SWM [single white male], young 66, hiker, N\S\D [nonsmoker, nondrinker], 5'9". Seeks caring younger SWF. Photo. Box 1234.

My researcher's blood stirred. I was "younger" and a "single white female." So I wrote. It would be an adventure.

My snapshot and note, on which I put my office address, drew a response with a photograph of the "handsome SWM" snapped at some reunion, with his arm around Pia Zadora. He wore a Jimmy Carter grin, but his face, close to the young singer's, was jowly, skin loose, eyes puffy. I had not the slightest urge to meet him, but in the interests of research, I called him.

He seemed pleased to hear from me and spoke for a long time about his hobbies and his hiking. He advertised regularly in the personals columns and knew the ropes. When I told him I had never done this before, he snapped back, "That's what they all say!" We arranged to meet in the cafeteria of the county museum of art.

I recognized him from his photo, even without the ear-to-ear grin. He looked tired, his features slightly droopy. His eyes avoided mine when we shook hands; he seemed ill at ease, despite his considerable experience in meeting women this way.

Perhaps he had been handsome once, but Box 1234 was not actually hiking these days and was getting stout. His hobby was, or rather had been, photography, and he brought some expertly matted prints to show me, pictures taken years, even decades, before.

The museum exhibit was fascinating, but I came away from the meeting saddened, not for myself but at the illusion that allowed this man to get through his days, the illusion that somewhere out there is a woman thirty or forty years his junior who is going to be bowled over and happy to be bedded by this ordinary, aging man. "Younger" in his advertisement meant a lot younger, it turned out. The most recent "girl" in his life, he told me, had been twenty-eight years old. Startled, I asked—rudely, I realized as I heard my words hanging in the air—"Why would any young person want . . .?

Reading Advertisement Codes

Lesson number one: Recognize the codes in advertisements and know how to read them! "Younger" probably means "young." "Active" may mean "be in good shape or don't bother."

Usually, a legend accompanies the personals pages, and some abbreviations, like the ones Box 1234 used, are fairly easy to make out. (I've seen WW mean "widow" or "widowed" or "white widower" or "white widow," and sometimes the word is partly spelled out: WDW or WDWR.)

Marital Status: **D**ivorced, **S**ingle, **WW**idow(er)
Sex: **F**emale, **M**ale
Religion: **C**hristian, **J**ewish
Ethnicity or Race: **A**sian, **B**lack, **H**ispanic, **W**hite
Sexual Preference: **G**ay, **L**esbian

Other abbreviations may require a bit of thought, for example:

ISO means "in search of."
LTR means "long-term relationship."

If you live in a large city, advertisers may include their residential area, such as WS (West Side) or OC (Orange County). The paper or magazine will carry explanations of these codes. Occasionally, an advertiser will make up his own abbreviations. I puzzled for a long time over SOH—and learned it was "sense of humor" only when I asked the man directly.

Newspaper Datelines

Much of the following discussion focuses on personal advertisements that appear in newspapers and magazines and that involve 900 telephone numbers. Some magazines use box number addresses that preserve the anonymity of the advertiser; respondents write to the advertisers in care of the box number. Still other magazines allow the flexibility of both 900 telephone numbers and box numbers. These kinds of daily and weekly newspaper advertisements carry different titles, including "Datelines," "Personals," "Telepersonals," "Relationship Ads," and so on.

Once unthinkable for respectable folks, personal advertisements in city and local newspapers are a major dating resource. Advertising is now among the most accepted and acceptable ways of meeting members of the opposite sex.

A measure of safety is built into this method because you have the opportunity to screen the people before you meet them. For extra assurance, you will, of course, set up the first meeting in a public place and will not invite a stranger into your home until you are sure the person poses no danger to you. And you won't let that wonderful mystery novel *Loves Music, Loves to Dance*, by Mary Higgins Clark, deter you!

In that book, a serial murderer finds his victims through newspaper personals! This made for an exciting story, but if you are sensible and cautious, you are in no more danger from a person you meet through a newspaper advertisement than from a person met in any other way.

The mechanics of using datelines (telephone) personals vary from newspaper to newspaper. The *Los Angeles Times* and many other city newspapers allow you to place an advertisement of up to four lines for no charge. (See inset on pages 48–49 for sample personals.) The ad appears for a stipulated number of insertions, perhaps two, perhaps four. You call in or mail your advertisement a week or so in advance of the first insertion and are given a box number and a personal code. You then call an 800 number, again at no charge, and record a voice message. The message can be heard by anyone who responds to your advertisement by calling your box number on a 900 line. Calling 900 numbers is expensive, and you can run up huge telephone bills if you are not careful! This is how the newspaper, or the sponsor of the personals pages, profits from the service.

The recorded message you leave for callers may last up to one minute and is censored! No sexually suggestive remarks are allowed, nor may you leave your surname or your address. You will ask the caller to leave a message, including his phone number, and you may then call *him*, if you so choose.

SOME SAMPLE PERSONALS

These personals may give you a taste of the kinds of advertisements placed by some over-fifties in one newspaper as well as some ideas for developing your own advertisement.

Women Seeking Men

Symphony, science, art, and having coffee with you. Sweet, pretty, prof[essional] DJF seeks educ affectionate N\S WM 50s.

Beautiful loving caring SF. ISO SWM, 50-65. With sense of humor, zest for life, marriage minded.

Serve and volley with this dynamic, slim, attractive DBF. Meet me at the net, the theater, the beach, or the movies if you are an active, quality SBM, 50-60, ready to follow through in a romantic game of singles or doubles.

Wanted, a special 56-60 WM who still likes Disneyland, old movies, dancing slow, the family, and grandchildren.

Grandma looking for grandpa. Must be 60+. Please give me a call.

Take a chance, Life's a gamble, anyway, and you might win the heart of a large, good-hearted lady. U: 50-65 with same qualities.

Classy chassis, low mileage\hi performance. SF loaded with extras. Romantically designed 4 SM, fin-sec [financially secure]. 50-64.

Faithful Penelope longs for her Odysseus; beautifully, artfully, joyously, patiently waiting 4 the love that endures.

Outstandingly beautiful, marvelous, charming, and above all modest DF ISO n\s companion.

Men Seeking Women

1932 New Yorker, well maintained like 57 model, trim, white, 66", grt lks [great looks] and body style. Lifetime warranty.

Retired college professor, SWM, special, sks loving intel shapely lady, 55-65, for mutual life enhancement.

Attractive fit DWM, 57, smoker, likes travel, romantic evenings, ISO slim, attractive WF lifemate to 63.

61, witty, lover of movies, music, animals, and travel. Seeks slim N\S lady to 55 to share life.

Tall, shy SBM, retired. Seeks Caribbean lady to share richness of life and love.

Grow old disgracefully. Celebrate the delights. DWM 59. N\S.

Widower, 65+, Christian Scientist. ISO one with same understanding.

Caring SWM. 60, engineer. Enjoys art, good music. ISO SWF, 50-56, trim, ready for romantic monog[amous] rel[ationship].

If *you* are responding to a printed advertisement, you will call the 900 number, leave a brief message and your telephone number, and wait for him to call you. Don't get carried away! The system is set up so that it takes time to complete the process. And if you call two or three or more numbers, you may have to take out a bank loan to meet the bill! Be selective!

My city's newspaper personals also list "Men Seeking Men" and "Women Seeking Women"—so there's something for everyone!

Magazine and Journal Personals

As well as newspaper datelines, magazines and journals specializing in subjects that interest you are good resources and will bring responses from people with whom you know you will have something in common. For someone interested in liberal politics, a magazine like *The Nation* may be suitable. People with certain religious or ethnic interests may be found in the pages of, for instance, *The Jewish Journal*.

Not all magazines carry personals, but this is a growing trend as it brings in revenues for the publishers. Most cities have at least one upscale magazine with pages set aside for singles, and a number of the men and women I have interviewed have used them successfully. See the inset on this page for a list of just a few magazines and newspapers that carry personal ads.

Advertising in these magazines is expensive, and they don't give free space as do some newspapers. They usually charge by the word with a minimum number of words. On the other hand, responding to such an advertisement may cost no more than a postage stamp as they, unlike many newspapers, offer the option of responding by mail.

MAGAZINES AND NEWPAPERS THAT CARRY PERSONAL ADS

Personal advertisements are carried by hundreds of magazines and newspapers across the country. Some have a national readership. Others are local. Just a few are listed here:

Boston	*New Age Journal*
Chicago	*New York*
Harper's Magazine	*The New York Review*
Interrace	*of Books*
The Jewish Journal	*Pittsburgh*
(Los Angeles)	*The Progressive*
Los Angeles	*Psychology Today*
Mother Jones	*Senior Life*
The Nation	*Southern Sierran*

Meeting a Friend Through the Personals

As always, and for the pleasure of their wit, I scanned the advertisements in *The New York Review of Books*. My husband and I used to read them aloud to each other:

Man with superb legs seeks woman with superb bosom . . .

Rajasthan? Turkey? Ecuador? This fall? DWF, light 50s, looking for man (5'9", 40-60) who wants to go on these and other journeys through life. Be happy. Be solvent, and we'll be on our way.

Most of the advertisers were based in New York, but one read:

Retired professor seeks intelligent, shapely woman to share conversation, nature, arts, travel. Los Angeles.

"Retired" might mean *recently* retired—someone of, say, sixty-five or sixty-six? I took courage and called the number listed. Most people list a box number, but this man's home number was given. I mentioned my recent widowhood on his answering machine and left my telephone number.

My husband had died less than a year before, but this man, I learned, was even more newly bereft than I. His wife had been killed only five months before by a hit-and-run driver as they had crossed the road together. A mathematician, he'd been retired for two years, he told me on the phone, which meant, I supposed, he was about sixty-seven.

We would have lunch the following day at a well-known restaurant in my neighborhood near my house. He arrived exactly on time, a beanpole of a man, so tall he seemed to veer slightly to one side. He looked frail—small wonder given his circumstances. After a while, his personality shone through, a nice, funny man, in terrible emotional pain.

Back at my house after lunch—my daughter was at home that day so I felt comfortable inviting him to my home to continue our conversation—he promptly asked if he could put his head down for half an hour! A sign of his age and emotional state, perhaps? I put him in the guest room with a pillow and went off to write letters.

He awoke refreshed, in no hurry to leave, so we sat in the garden until evening, with him planning to come back early the next day to walk around Hollywood Lake with me. At last, he left, not before giving me a big hug at the bottom of the steps. It felt good—the first hug I'd had for a long time. A fine and decent man, I thought, but I was troubled by his years. By now, I was estimating somewhere in the mid-seventies.

My daughter and I talked together about the importance of age. She dismissed it as a non-issue: "What counts, Mum, is physical and emotional age, not the number of years a person has lived." She was right, of course. We all know a few "old men" in their forties. If a person is active, in good health, living for today, and thinking about tomorrow and the next day, his chronological age is not important.

The mathematician had a fascinating past, having worked on the development of the atomic bomb. I hung on his every word, like a schoolgirl, as he talked of the famous physicists he'd known—Fermi, Oppenheimer, Feynman—and the ethical problems he'd had with nuclear power.

I could really get to like this man, I thought, after several outings with him, but with my gradual warming came his increasing depression. So soon after his tragedy, it was too early for a new relationship. His depression deepened, and in empathy, my spirits dropped too, as I was reminded of my own loss. This was not good for me, I decided. We would remain casual friends.

That friendship, which is now deep and solid, has sustained us both through some trying times. Good friends are precious, so don't overlook the possibility that while a person you meet through a personal advertisement may not turn out to be the man of your romantic dreams, he may become important to you in other ways, widening your circle of friends and enriching your life.

Placing My Own Advertisements

As I had made a good friend through following an advertisement in *The New York Review of Books*, I inserted my own personal advertisement, giving a box number and requesting a photograph. It drew three responses. I had stipulated "55-65" as the age range of interest, but two of the respondents turned out to be substantially older. One, interesting on paper, was, or rather had been, a music critic, particularly knowledgeable about chamber music, one of my passions. He described himself as "handsome" and invited me to a concert.

By no stretch of the imagination could "George" be called handsome. The rather blurred snapshot he had sent me either was of someone else or had been taken a long time ago. We got off to a rough start as he got lost on his way to our meeting place and then got lost on the way to the concert hall, so we missed the entire first half of the program. Once at the concert, he spoke to me only occasionally as he knew several people in the crowd, hailed them noisily, and held them unwilling captives with stories of who was playing what music where, while I stood on the fringes wishing I were somewhere else. He did, finally, introduce me to some of his acquaintances, charming people, almost any one of whom I would rather have been with that evening! He got lost yet again, on the way back. We drove in relative silence, knowing we would not meet again.

Another respondent to my advertisement met me at a beach restaurant for coffee; he spoke of himself as "the most reluctant bachelor around." Sophisticated, Italian-born, "Luigi" was blasé about the dating scene. He had been on the "quest" for a partner for a very long time. He had waited until he was forty-two to wed and was divorced after only eight years. Now, in his upper sixties, he was wary about another commitment.

When I spoke of my full life and my good fortune in having the support of friends and family, he indicated he had heard all these phrases before and saw them as "codes." His response was sharp: "Perhaps you don't need to venture out, given such a full life!"

Luigi and his men friends were experienced at dating through the personals, and he confirmed my observations about the way people describe themselves.

"The men all advertise themselves as younger than they really are. They say they are taller and better-looking than they really are. You have to get the women to meet you before you can impress them; but a woman has to be disappointed in the reality," he said.

"Perhaps that *is* the reality for them," I suggested, noting that, despite his protestations about the foolishness of lying, he had understated his own age.

Luigi called me a few weeks later, charming and courtly. He didn't want me to think he hadn't liked me, but "a lady from long ago" had returned to his life. He was eager to tell me that I was "Lovely! Perfect!" and to keep meeting people and having fun. He may, or may not, have been telling the truth about the lady from the past. I later learned from some of my interviewees that this is a fairly common device used, mostly by women, to gently let down men they don't want to see any more!

The return from my first advertisement being sparse, I inserted an advertisement in *The Nation*, a magazine to which I had long subscribed. It, too, is published in New York with a national circulation appealing to those politically left of center and relatively intellectual. Here, I struck the mother lode! The response was overwhelming; some twenty men answered, including three Ph.D.s and two M.D.s. Most were from my city, as I had given my hometown in the advertisement, but a few were from other parts of the state, one even from the East Coast.

I did as Luigi suggested. I met most of them and had such a hectic social life, I got hardly any work done!

The Nation was so good a resource, I couldn't wait to tell my older, single women friends. Two of them placed personal advertisements and had similar responses to mine. In fact, a few of the same men who'd written to me also wrote to them!

It's fun to recall being wooed with fruit by one of *The Nation* men! A university colleague, enchanted when she heard about it, asked, "Does he bring you mangoes and guavas and exotic things like that?" "No," I said. "Just citrus; it isn't a metaphor for anything. It's just fruit."

The "fruit man" did, in fact, propose marriage—over the top of a bag of grapefruits. It was the first serious proposal I'd had, and I seriously considered it—for about a minute and a half. It took me only that long to realize I was too recently widowed to make such a commitment. Also, I was having too interesting a time to settle down just yet!

The number of responses to personal advertisements and the suitability of respondents will vary from advertisement to advertisement. Men I have interviewed tell me they are sometimes swamped with a hundred calls or more. At other times, only three or four women will respond. Some of my advertisements in our local newspaper, the *Los Angeles Times*, have yielded ten or twelve responses, others brought only one or two—or none. So, don't take it personally or feel yourself a "failure" if your advertisement doesn't draw many—or any—responses. The "success" rate seems to vary randomly for everyone, and you may have many more responses to the next advertisement you place.

The men who have answered have included a newly widowed, internationally famous psychiatrist (an instantly recognizable name in academic circles), a building contractor, a hairdresser, a university professor, a physician-artist, a union organizer, several businessmen, and many retired men from a wide range of professions.

Iris's Story

One of my friends, "Iris," is now seriously involved with a man she met through *The Nation's* personals column; they are talking of marriage as he prepares to move to the West Coast from his eastern city. They began their courtship through the mail and long, cross-country telephone calls. Even before they met face to face, they felt a real affinity for each other. Finally, "Louis" travelled to Los Angeles for a long weekend, staying at a hotel near Iris's apartment.

The romance blossomed quickly, both feeling the pressure of the geographical distance between them and the need to make the most of every moment together. After Louis visited twice more, he decided to move across the country. The old cliché still applies: Love can overcome obstacles, even courtship across three thousand miles.

FOLLOWING UP ON A PERSONAL AD

Before you decide to meet a respondent in person, you will first talk to him on the telephone. Your telephone conversation will help you decide whether you would like to know him better.

The Initial Telephone Conversation

The telephone call is the first filter of the screening process after you have responded to someone's advertisement, or he has responded to yours. Now you can talk as long as you wish at no cost, or relatively little cost, depending on local charges. You can gather a fair amount of information about him and decide if you want to meet him or not.

The safest areas to ask about are work and hobbies and the place where he grew up and went to school. You can find out his tastes in music and the arts, his background, and so on. You might also talk about his children.

You can probe a little into his marital history, although some tact is needed here. People may take offense at being asked really personal questions like "Have you been involved in any relationships since becoming single?" A rule of thumb here is to ask yourself how *you* would feel if you were asked that kind of question. Nevertheless, you will want to know if a man is still angry or bitter about a divorce, or if he is grieving deeply. You may want to be sure that he is, indeed, unattached romantically!

You will also want to try to discern if he is basically a cheerful, forward-looking person or a grouch. Does he drone on and on about himself, or does he seem genuinely interested in knowing about you. In short, is this a person you would like to spend some time with?

Sometimes, the initial telephone meeting is so delightful that it continues for an hour or more. The two of you develop a real rapport and look forward to meeting in person. But he is still a blind date, and you may—or may not—be disappointed in the flesh and blood reality. It's an adventure! And all that is lost is a little of your time.

From time to time, you'll speak to someone who may have had a terrible day and who projects all his frustrations on you!

A man, "Jack," left a message in my voice-mail box. I called back, only to find him so touchy that pleasant conversation was impossible.

"What kind of work do you do?" I asked—a usual and, you'd think, fairly nonthreatening question.

"I'm an art teacher."

"That's wonderful!" I said, genuinely interested. "Where do you teach?"

For some reason, this question made him angry.

"What does it matter where I teach?" he snapped. "Would I be more loveable if I taught at Harvard than if I taught at some other place?"

"I'm sorry," I said. "Where you teach isn't really significant. It's just that I teach too, and I thought we might teach at the same place."

When I said I had been happily married, he came back with "The longer you're a widow, the more wonderful and saintly your husband will become. I know these things."

Straining to be polite, I talked a little about my work and interests.

"If you have such a rich life," he said, "why are you advertising for a man?"

Finally, exasperated, I suggested that he was obviously tired of responding to these kinds of question and seemed to have a bit of an "attitude."

That made him *really* angry. "How rude of you! How rude! All you have to say is you don't think we have much in common and goodbye."

"Okay," I sighed. "I don't think we have much in common, Jack. Goodbye."

As I hung up the phone, feeling rather mean and rude, I realized that I should have excused myself from the encounter earlier. Instead of trying to deal with this man's odd responses to what I thought were reasonable questions, I should have protected myself from the discomfort he caused me and from the wasted effort of making conversation that was going nowhere. So, if you ever find yourself in a similar situation, you might remind yourself that you don't have to serve as psychoanalyst to strange people!

The First Meeting

A first meeting with a stranger—and the man *is* a stranger, even if you've spoken on the telephone many times and feel as though you know him—should be in a public place with other people around. Most people choose to meet for coffee, usually in the midmorning, in daylight, at a coffee house or restaurant that one or the other knows well or one that is easily reached by both of you. The advantage of the coffee meeting is that it can be brief—but need not be—and a cup of coffee is a minor expenditure compared to luncheon or dinner.

If both people are working during the day, they may choose to meet for lunch at a centrally placed restaurant, or if they work in different parts of the city, coffee on a Saturday or Sunday morning may be the answer. This is clearly something to be worked out for the convenience of both the people involved.

Be prepared for the first meeting to be the last. You may simply not like the look of the person, he may not be taken with you, or you may be mutually disappointed. On the other hand, you may become so engrossed with each other's conversation that morning coffee stretches into lunch and into dinner. And then the movies.

I have had both kinds of experiences. One man I met for morning coffee got down to brass tacks immediately. He said, "I must have sex with any new woman within two weeks; there's no point in wasting time. The sex has to be right, or there's no point in continuing. Time is not on my side."

Seeing my horrified expression, he told me I would never get married if I wasn't prepared to "live life." "You'll still be looking in ten years' time, and every day the merchandise is losing value! All you'll be able to find will be old men who are ill!" He was equally outspoken about the need to "keep the juices flowing" by having sex. "Use it or lose it!"

Feeling physically nauseated by his hateful words, I jumped up from the table, uneaten croissant in hand, ran to my car, and sped off as fast as I could! This, I told myself, is one of the jerks people keep telling me are out there!

Fortunately, few of the men I met were jerks. They were mostly well-mannered, pleasant people, and even if we didn't arrange another meeting, we passed an enjoyable hour or two of good conversation. Chapter 6 gives details about safety precautions you should be sure to take.

First Meeting Talk

The conversation at that first meeting, men tell me, is better if it doesn't get too personal. "She told me she'd been clinically depressed and had tried to commit suicide on three occasions. Honestly, I didn't need to know that! Not yet. Then, she asked me if I'd like her to go home with me. I didn't think so! I've got too many knives and things around. . . ."

It is probably not a good idea to talk about your ex-husband and the circumstances of your divorce, either, at this early stage. I must confess I am put off right away when a man starts bad-mouthing his ex-wife, so I can see that men might feel the same way.

Other topics best avoided when you first meet—and these include recommendations given to me by several professional matchmakers—are your health problems, your financial problems, your niggling workplace disputes, serious worries about your children, or your longing to be married! You know yourself that upbeat people are much more fun to be with than complainers, so keep it light.

This meeting is an opportunity for you to get to know enough about the man to see if you care to meet him again, and to present yourself in a positive way. That doesn't mean you must play-act or pretend to be someone you are not. Listen as much as you talk. Expand on your earlier telephone conversation. Ask the man where he grew up. Does he like his job? Has he traveled recently? What kinds of films does he like? Does he have children? Let him tell you about them, if he wants to.

It is always a little awkward to make conversation with someone you haven't met before, but if you are alert to what is going on in the world, you will find something to talk about: the latest hit movie; the Oscars; the Emmys; current happenings; the latest food fads; books; sports. Glance through the morning newspaper or the latest news magazine for some ideas before you set off for the meeting, just in case you run out of topics.

Both of you may be nervous, trying so hard to make a good impression that you go babbling on. You don't have to tell your entire life story right now. Nor do you have to take the meeting too seriously. It's just coffee, not an emotional commitment!

Who Pays? The New Etiquette

As a professional, I am used to paying my own way. Dinner with colleagues, male or female, usually means splitting the bill, and no one feels uncomfortable about it. But what do you do when meeting a man for the first time over lunch or a snack? The offer to pay for yourself is sometimes received gratefully; lots of people are living on fixed incomes and eating out is a luxury. Most often, the offer is dismissed with a wave of the hand and "No, I wouldn't hear of it!"

Once, when I told my lunch companion, "Rick," that I was conducting research for a book on dating in later life, as I usually did at some point during a first meeting, the man was indignant. "I never allow a lady to pay for her meal, but if this is business for you, it's quite legitimate!" Fair enough.

Sure I would never hear from him again, I was surprised when, some four months later, he called. "I hope you've finished work on your book by now. I would really like to see you again, but I don't want to be one of your research subjects." I had to look through my notes to remind myself who he was! He insisted on paying for dinner the next time, by the way. And for the theater.

Most of the men I met were fascinated with my research topic and eager to tell me their experiences as singles—and they usually bought lunch too! They tell me it isn't usual for women to offer to pay their way, but they do appreciate it when it happens, even if they don't accept.

Not only do most women not offer to share the food tab, but some also deter the men with their extravagant demands. A nice fellow with whom I shared Sunday brunch at the beach told me of a woman at a first meeting who chided him about the restaurant he had chosen: "Honestly, it was a good eatery, but she complained `You could have taken me *anywhere*; what made you pick this place?'" You can bet he never asked her out again.

Men do not like to feel they are being taken advantage of. A dear old friend, who had been looking for the "right lady" for some time, often shared some of the details of his dates with me. He arranged to meet a woman at noon. "I don't bother with first meeting for coffee any more," he said. "Might as well have lunch. It seems more substantial, somehow."

The woman, who happened to be French, insisted that they eat at a French restaurant she knew. "John," my friend, was agreeable—and then he saw the menu, and the exorbitant prices!

"I couldn't believe what she ordered. The most expensive dish she could find, and a daiquiri before the meal, and an elaborate dessert afterwards. I didn't like her much anyway, and I could see she was aiming to get a super meal at my expense. So I told her we were going Dutch—something I never do. She was really taken aback, but she paid up!"

Who pays for what requires negotiation these days; the old rules of etiquette apply some of the time but not all the time. Young people and business people take sharing costs for granted, while some older women tell me, "A real gentleman pays to take a lady out." You have to use your judgment and a measure of tact.

Love at First Sight

Forget it! That's my sincere recommendation to you. I hear lots of talk about chemistry and electricity between people as their eyes meet across a crowded room. Yes, people can take an instant liking to each other, but don't be disappointed—and don't give up on the person—if that chemistry doesn't make itself felt at a first meeting. Indeed, if there are flashes of lightning when you shake hands, be prepared for the storm to fizzle out pretty quickly.

For your own sake, please be realistic about this. Don't let someone walk away just because that initial spark is missing. He might be perfect for you if you give him a chance.

USING PERSONALS TO ORGANIZE SINGLES EVENTS

An interesting way of using personal advertisements is to invite single people in your preferred age group to a mix-and-match gathering or party or evening out. Here is an actual advertisement from a New York magazine:

We are 7 women looking for 7 men to join us for a dinner party. We are as diverse and as interesting as we'd like each of you to be. We are, and are looking for men who are, fun-loving, 50-plus, attractive, intelligent, emotionally healthy, financially secure, nonsmokers with a sense of humor. Individuals please send photo with note.

The advertisers have made very clear the kind of men they are looking for. Letters and photographs will help them screen the men. They will surely follow up with phone calls before making their final selection.

Given seven men and seven women who begin with some interests in common, the chances are good that some of them will find agreeable matches. At the very least, they'll all have an enjoyable evening and a good meal!

If you can't find six women friends prepared to go along with you on organizing a dinner party, think of other kinds of evening or afternoon events. These could be concert or theater outings for, say, three men and three women. A personal advertisement in the "Mutual Interests" or the "50-Plus" section of the newspaper personals pages might find both the men and the women to make up the group.

For example, an advertisement taken directly from my local paper reads as follows: "Single golfer seeking other single golfers to fill out some foursomes on 18-hole courses." Another suggests organizing a group of men and women to attend a museum together, followed by a meal at a nearby restaurant. Docent-led tours, regularly scheduled at most major museums, provide a good framework for this kind of activity. Other advertisers seek "like-minded men and women to get together at coffee houses and other venues to listen to, or play, acoustic music" or "on-fire M/F Christians, any race, for prayers, discussions, and Bible study." The possibilities are limited only by your imagination.

MEETING ON-LINE

How bizarre! That is still the reaction of lots of men and women of all ages to the idea of "dating in cyberspace." Yet, on-line services have been with us for many years now. Some users run home-based businesses from their desk and laptop computers. You can buy airline tickets, pay your bills, send faxes and e-mail letters, book your vacations, take university courses, research the stock market—and on and on—from your computer. So why not look for love on the computer too?

My friend "Holly," in her fifties, met the man she has been seeing for the past eighteen months by way of the Internet, and one of *her* friends is marrying her cyberspace match next month. I learned, too, that Rush Limbaugh, the conservative political commentator, met his third wife on-line. This wave of the future is already here!

To those who aren't familiar with these electronic advances, all of this seems pretty scary. If you are interested in plunging into this new arena, though, why not look at any of the dozens of books on the subject or take a course at your local community college or through adult education? You'll learn about on-line dating and a whole lot more.

If you are already on-line, the following information will probably be familiar to you. It is offered here to give courage to those who have yet to get their feet wet.

You will, of course, need a computer, and it must have a modem. The modem allows you to plug into a telephone line through which you access your on-line service.

On-line services, unless you are associated with a university or a government organization or some similar group, carry a monthly charge. This fee will give you five hours or so on-line without extra cost. Once you use up that time, you will be charged for each additional hour of use.

Increasingly, on-line companies are offering more hours, even unlimited hours, of services for a somewhat higher monthly fee. The field is changing so rapidly that it is difficult to assess whether this arrangement will eventually become standard or if options will still be available. Be aware that heavy use of on-line services charged by the hour can run up huge bills. I've known people to spend hundreds of dollars a month, not realizing how much time they were sitting at their screens. There is something hypnotic about computers!

You can "meet" people on-line just as you meet them through personal advertisements in newspapers and magazines. You look for people who share your interests and values.

When you start communicating, you are, according to those who use these services, "inside each other's head." Many cyberspace users find their on-line friends much easier to talk to than people in the same room. The medium seems to allow an outpouring of heart and soul that is less possible in ordinary meeting places. This is probably because the other person is really anonymous, hiding behind an on-screen "name."

"I can't believe I'm telling you this. I've never talked about this to anyone before" is the kind of statement often made on-line.

I am told you can easily "fall in love" with your cyberspace friend after communicating for a period of time without ever having met him in the flesh.

You are, of course, falling in love with an image—perhaps not even an image but rather a "mind merge." It's a fantasy, which may simply disappear when you meet in person. Or it may not.

Phyllis's Story

"Phyllis," another person who initially met her fiancé on-line, found even speaking on the telephone to "Ian" a strange and unnerving experience after communicating only on the screen.

"Ian is really `strong' when he talks on-line. When he speaks in person though, he is much . . . meeker. It was a difficult transition."

Ian lived on the West Coast, Phyllis in New York. The two arranged to meet in New York three months after their first computer conversation.

"We really knew a great deal about each other," Phyllis told me. "We had told each other more than most people say in a lifetime." Still, had the two met in any other way, she says, it's unlikely they would have given each other the time of day: Ian is a smoker; Phyllis hates everything about cigarettes.

Phyllis is tall; Ian is short. Ian says he would have been intimidated by Phyllis, a successful, independent, professional woman, if he hadn't had the opportunity to get "inside her head" before he met her.

Ian has now relocated to a small town on the edge of New York and commutes to visit Phyllis. He has reduced his smoking to a couple of cigarettes a day and hopes to have given it up completely before the two marry.

Using On-Line Services

Any of the commercial services, such as America Online (AOL), CompuServe, Prodigy, and Microsoft Network, will give you access to on-line dating. The more you experiment on-line, the more familiar you will become with the range of possibilities. You can even speak on-line with people in other countries at no extra cost.

Just to start: the opening screen of AOL will show, among other options, "Life Styles and Interests." If you click on that heading with your mouse, you will then be given lists of other choices, including "Senior Net Online." Once there, you can leave a message—a personal advertisement—or you can read other people's messages and respond to them. Other options include "Love @ AOL," "Cyberpals," and all kinds of "chat rooms" that you choose to join because the subject being discussed interests you. You can check through "Hobbies," "Religion," and "AARP [American Association for Retired Persons]," which also provide message boards, ways to leave and receive messages. The possibilities are endless; new features are constantly being added.

You can also click onto "Internet Connection" and "World Wide Web," and search out all the computer addresses that have to do with the topic of interest. For instance, I entered "Love Online" as my search topic and learned there were over seventeen thousand documents available! I then requested the first fifty of those and printed them out. They included "Web Match Personals Singles Romance Ads Advertising," "Love Online—A Practical Guide to Digital Dating," "Finding True Love . . . Online," and "Web Personals." Some of the descriptions hinted at decidedly raunchy content; you will soon learn to filter the material.

For the serious searcher for love in cyberspace, the refinements can include putting your photograph on-line. Anyone who likes the picture will be able to call up your personal profile on which you will have entered your tastes and values. If a person is interested in knowing you better, he will be able to leave you a message, and if you wish, you'll be able to check his personal profile before you reply. Putting pictures on-line requires some extra software: an art viewer or photo viewer and a program such as Thumbs Plus or an addition to Microsoft's Paintbrush. Some of this software is "freeware;" some carries a small monthly fee.

A very slightly risqué photo put on line by Holly, the friend I mentioned earlier, was accessed by nearly two thousand men; hundreds of messages followed. Eventually, she met three or four of the men with whom she had been corresponding by computer and telephone before settling into her present relationship.

You will make your own decisions about using computer dating as a resource. Clearly, men and women do meet this way and find love, but you may or may not be comfortable with the technology or with the need to filter the serious seekers from the "nuts and berries" on-line.

A membership in an on-line service is a bit like membership in a club, the club offering thousands of activities in hundreds of rooms. Some activities you may find distasteful—such as near-pornography and "dirty talk" and "cybersex"—part of the reason people are concerned about what their children are looking at when they are supposed to be doing their homework on the computer! Members of the club are not screened as they are before they can join some other kinds of clubs. You will have to do the screening yourself.

Finally, if you do want to meet someone off-line—in person—all the same precautions (described in Chapter 6) apply as when meeting any stranger. Meet in a public place—and so on.

You've worked your way through a lot of information about some ways of plunging directly into dating: personal advertisements in newspapers and magazines, organizing your own singles events, and meeting on-line. Pause and digest. There's more!

Chapter Four

Dating Services and Other Resources

G ood men, it seems, have always been hard to find, but
they *are* out there. The ways to look for them are many
and varied, direct and indirect. So far, I have suggested
that personal advertisements—a very direct method of looking
for compatible members of the opposite sex—work well for
many people. Now I'll give you my recommendations, the pros
and the cons, based on my experience and research, of some
other direct methods: dating services and matchmakers, dances
and socials, and singles organizations, both commercial and
noncommercial.

DATING SERVICES AND MATCHMAKERS

Before I became a widow, I hardly noticed the profusion of advertisements for dating and matchmaking services. I had heard
about video dating, and I recall a particularly poignant episode of
the television show *thirtysomething*, still played on rerun channels.
Two of the women characters, anxious about the ticking of their
biological clocks and eager to marry, sign up to be video-
matched. They giggle with embarrassment as they perform for
the camera—and then flip through the pages of available men.

Several of these companies have called me and some of my interviewees to offer their services, probably because we have placed advertisements in personals columns. Lists of singles seem to circulate among businesses catering to this huge group. In Los Angeles, for instance, there are roughly 1.6 million unmarried adults; the figures are proportionately high in other cities. My name, it seems, is on several lists.

How Dating and Matchmaking Services Work

One day a woman called me from a singles club offering video library, personal library, background checks on clients, and so on. ("Personal library" refers to books, as opposed to video-tapes, filled with photographs and information about single men and women looking for partners or dates.)

"Come in and look through the videos and the information," she cooed. "You'll feel like a kid in a candy store when you see all the wonderful men you can choose among!"

I'm sure she had no idea of my age. Video dating works best, if it works at all well, for younger people. Men who have joined video dating services have told me of their disappointment in the small number of older women on the books. Being picked from a book of photographs or from a videotape does not seem a particularly appealing way for older people to meet each other. The picture books are filled with pretty young girls and handsome young men, and older people may not feel comfortable with the idea of being chosen by their looks. Perhaps if some enterprising business people ran a service, or a branch of their service, exclusively for the over-fifties, people in this age range would be more accepting.

In any case, dating services—which are just what they say: services that arrange dates, not necessarily matches or marriages—can be expensive. One agency, for instance charges several hundred dollars a year for a passive membership: The member's picture is entered into the books, and other people have the option of selecting him or her. The passive member cannot select anyone. The cost of an active membership begins at well over a thousand dollars—and these charges can change at any time. An active member can pick, and be picked, from books and videos.

A "picked" member is sent a card indicating that someone is interested in him or her. He or she may then decide whether or not to meet the one who has done the selecting. A visit to the office will give more information and a look at the interested party's picture and files. As with personal advertisements, the couple talks on the telephone before deciding about meeting.

Matchmakers are of another order of service and, usually, far more expensive than dating services. Matchmakers claim to find partners—people who want long-term relationships or marriage—and couples are supposedly individually matched for interests, hobbies, religion, goals and values, age, appearance requirements, personality, and so on.

A couple of years before my husband died, when I had no personal interest in the information, my dental hygienist had diverted my attention from her probing by fascinating me with her story of meeting her husband through the "VNP Club" (not its real name), a matchmaking organization for Jewish singles. VNP advertised regularly in my local newspaper so, now single, I called the number, received a package of information through the mail, completed the application form, and sent it in. After several weeks of not hearing, I called. The proprietor didn't remember my application, but she said she would be happy to meet me.

"I thought you considered me a hopeless case," I laughed.

"There are no hopeless cases," she insisted. "There's someone for everyone."

We arranged to meet at her office the following Tuesday at eleven in the morning.

Carefully dressed, I set off for the meeting feeling embarrassed, silly, and very much aware of my years and the strange circumstances. I arrived a bit early and found the door to the VNP office locked. After a cup of coffee in a nearby café, I went back at exactly eleven o'clock. The door was still locked. I waited. And waited. At noon, I pushed a note under the door and went home. As if it weren't weird enough to be investigating a dating service at my age and in my station, being stood up by the matchmaker was surely an indignity of high order.

Follow-up calls to the VNP office were never returned; no explanation was ever given. I could have assumed that this agency *did* deem my case hopeless, but I am nothing if not persistent in the cause of science. More likely, I decided, this was simply a poorly run, understaffed, and disorganized operation, and I must try others for a truer picture of the matchmaking business.

Recruitment Practices

Undeterred by my experience, I did speak with proprietors of several other matchmaking services to learn what they offered and whether they were worth their fees.

The most expensive service I came across was termed "the Rolls-Royce of matchmakers" in videotape clips of television programs shown during a presentation to potential clients. This service included a psychological evaluation, with a Rorschach test, as part of the preparation for making a match. Other advance work included a handwriting analysis; an evaluation of financial holdings; a private investigator's search to discover any criminal or prison record; a medical examination complete with a test for HIV or AIDS—and a horoscope based on date and time of birth! The clients also received several hours of one-on-one consultation with the matchmaker to get a clear picture of each client's requirements.

"I give them what they need, not what they want—and they forget what they wanted," said the proprietor of this establishment, who claimed to have matched six thousand couples in some twenty years of business.

In her waiting room, prior to interviewing the matchmaker, I spoke with one of the clients, a woman in her upper fifties.

"How long have you been with the service?" I asked.

"Just over two years."

"And have you been pleased?"

"Well, not really . . . but that may be my fault. I've had some problems, and I haven't been as interested in the search as I might have been."

"How much did the service cost you?" I asked, very nosey— but that's my job!

She hesitated before telling me.

"Twenty thousand dollars," she said.

I hope I managed to maintain my professional demeanor and that my jaw didn't drop too noticeably.

"What made you come to this agency?" I asked.

"Well, I kept seeing the ads in the paper, and when I called, they invited me to a seminar. She [the proprietor] is very persuasive, so I signed up."

I, too, had been invited to one of these seminars, held in a fancy hotel, when I first called the office for information about the service for my files. About 150 people paid the ten-dollar fee, which was waived for me as a guest of the agency. The ten dollars bought light refreshments and a motivational talk, given by the matchmaker herself, who made a dramatic entrance to wild applause after an impressively choreographed introduction by her elegant, beautifully dressed staff.

"I haven't time to provide my service for everyone who would benefit from it, so I am going to give you my secrets for finding a good match!" She presented us all with a book filled with her "secrets" on how to find "marriage material." These were largely sensible ways to build self-esteem—essential if a person is to talk comfortably and with confidence to strangers.

In reality, these "seminars" are a way to recruit new clients. Two days later, a telephone call invited me for a personal consultation with the matchmaker; my name and phone number had been taken from the application form filled out by everyone attending the seminar.

A long interview with a staff member at this matchmaker's office made clear the kinds of people who would pay $20,000— and more, *much* more—to have someone find them a spouse. (If you are the least bit cynical, you are probably saying something like, "That kind of person must be not too bright—and have more money than sense!")

"Our clients are all well-established, `together,' accomplished achievers who have everything—full lives—except someone to share it all with, and no time to do the kind of exploration you are doing for your book," the counselor told me. "They want someone to do that for them and are willing to pay that someone to cut through the weeks and months of finding out about a man or a woman's background."

Despite the very high prices she charged, this matchmaker gave no guarantees, claiming to find partners for about 60 percent of her clients. She was always looking for matches, she said, even in her leisure time.

"I'll approach a man in a restaurant if he looks likely for one of my clients. I went over to someone the other evening and asked him outright if he was married! `It's not your business!' he said. `That's where you're wrong,' I told him. `It *is* my business.'"

Interestingly, this very high-priced matchmaker closed up shop and left town not long after our meeting, under something of a cloud. Whether her clients ever got back any part of their paid-up-front fees is unknown. Perhaps they should have hired a private detective to investigate *her* before they invested their money in her service!

Because matchmakers are now so visible a part of the singles scene and because they recruit so aggressively, I examined several more before choosing two to investigate from inside as a client. At each of the agencies, I learned some fairly obvious snippets of dating wisdom from the resident psychologists and proprietors. For example:

§   "Lots of people have had bad experiences with members of the opposite sex. I tell them one bad meal doesn't mean all meals are going to be bad."

§   "People are not always ready for a new partner, still hung up on some old, unhealthy relationship. They say there are no good men (or women) out there and dating is boring. When they are ready, they find attractive people everywhere."

Most of the matchmakers I found work from elegant suites of offices in good commercial districts such as Beverly Hills and Century City in Los Angeles and similar areas in other cities. This alone makes for high overhead. Most provide a set number of matches for up to three years. Some offer lifetime services. Few make any promises. One owner, whose company boasts a "psychological director" to interview and test all the clients, says he is better at discerning who is *not* for you than who is. He charges several thousands of dollars and could give no success rate as he had not been in business long enough for this to be assessed.

I was directed to this particular office through one of my male interviewees, "Bill," who was recruited by the service after his personal advertisement appeared in an upscale city magazine. He, by the way, was charged no fee. He had to agree to a medical test, at his own cost, and psychological testing, and he is "on call" as a possible match for women clients interested in an over-seventy, healthy, educated man.

Don't Pay Too Much!

I did discover, too late for the health of my own pocketbook, that fees are sometimes negotiable or waived entirely for "desirable" clients such as Bill. Also, one or two free memberships are sometimes given away as prizes at recruiting seminars.

One matchmaker told me he has no set fee. After a consultation, the staff decides how difficult the client will be to match, and the fee is set accordingly. His costs ranged from three thousand dollars for a guaranteed number of matched introductions to twenty thousand dollars.

The staff at all these agencies are almost fawning in their handling of prospective clients—at least, until they've signed them up. Well-trained in flattery, they unfailingly made much of my hair, my eyes, my charm, my clothes, and anything else they could invent to speak of highly. Even in the elevator going up to one matchmaker's office, one of two staff people returning from lunch and guessing where I was headed, said to the other, "Oh, what a *lovely* lady that is!" It can be heady stuff, if you don't recognize it as part of the sales pitch.

A Tale of Two Matchmakers

For my investigation as a paying customer, I finally settled on one medium- to high-priced agency and one whose charges were so low, relatively, I wondered how the agency could stay in business. As it happens, it didn't!

The more expensive service—and we'll call it "Barbara Baker's Individual Search"—claimed to provide six possible matches within two years. If fewer than six were delivered, the proportionate amount of the fee would be refunded, unless their matchmaking was successful before the six matches were exhausted. The cheapie service—let's call it "Ladies First"—set no limits on numbers but would search for suitable partners for six months.

The Royal Treatment

First, why would a person with, say, an average middle-class income, lay out close to four thousand dollars, up front, on the chance of meeting "Mr. or Ms. Right" or even "Mr. or Ms. Not-Too-Wrong"? How did Barbara Baker present her agency as a worthwhile investment of such a sizable chunk of cash?

Her advertisements invited close inspection of the service: "Drop by the office for coffee and a chat. Come several times. No obligation."

As a potential client, I was greeted warmly by the office receptionist. Barbara Baker herself took time for a "getting to know you" chat, this conversation being almost entirely one-sided, devoted to Ms. Baker's enormous success and to the virtual singles "empire" she had founded. She had thousands of singles on her mailing lists, she said, and promoted parties and mixers all over the county.

"I don't recommend the parties for you," she insisted. "The men are too unsophisticated for a lady of your intellect—and," she added, peering into my face, "you deserve the best. You are a very pretty woman." I smiled to myself at this transparent flattery and at the obviously negative sales pitch. The parties cost very little to attend compared to the full-blown individual search, and she had a "live one" here who might sign up for the works.

A program director, "Janice," was then assigned to me to answer all my questions.

"I've heard,"—I was a bit sly—"that to meet contractual obligations some agencies use their own family members to make up the number of matches. How do I know you won't do that here?"

Janice appeared shocked. "We have no need," she assured me, "We have so many wonderfully eligible men in your age group. . . . Wait just a moment," she called over her shoulder as she ran out of the room, soon returning with a sheaf of files. "These are just the tip of the iceberg," she said, placing the stack on her desk. "Most of the men are currently being matched so their files aren't available. These are just a few for you to look at so you can see the caliber of men who sign up for our service."

She allowed me to look at several photographs of men in their fifties and sixties and read me information about their requirements and their incomes—not one making less than "a hundred thou. a year," she added.

"Do the men pay the same as the women?"

"Absolutely! Our men are serious about finding a life partner and are willing to pay. We have such a good reputation! We have successfully matched hundreds of couples. We are always thrilled when our clients marry."

I was still not persuaded to part with my money, full fee to be paid in advance, so Janice encouraged me to think about it before signing. I was to complete a short profile before I left the office so she could begin finding a suitable match; the longer, more detailed questionnaire I would answer at home.

"I've already got two or three wonderful men in mind for you," she tempted.

At our next meeting, Janice explained that the first introduction would be made within thirty days. After two months, another introduction would be made, and I could date both men if I wished. After two months more, unless I said "Hold it!" yet another man would be provided.

Services Rendered

A week or so later, for the high purposes of research, I bit the bullet, paid the fee, and prepared to write my report. Janice immediately abandoned me to "Fran," and I never saw or spoke to Janice again. Her job was done.

Fran, in her twenties, was a matchmaker, and together with Barbara Baker herself would use my detailed profile to find up to six suitable "gentlemen" over the course of the contract. Or so they said.

The profile, a list of personal characteristics and preferences, was drawn from a series of questions I had answered in detail. These concerned my tastes in music and the arts and the kinds of activities I enjoyed and would expect to share with another person: Did I like travel? sports? What did I enjoy reading? A number of questions concerned my temperament: Was I an extrovert or an introvert? Did I plan ahead, or was I more spontaneous? Was I romantic? religious? What was my preferred age range and level of education?

The kind of mate I sought had already been discussed at length with Janice; I assumed that information had been handed to Fran. It had not, but in any case, Fran, it seemed, was not to be my matchmaker for long. She was coming down with the flu, she thought, and she was getting married in less than a month and had important personal matters on her mind. Further, she'd had more experience with matching younger people and wasn't comfortable matching people in my age group.

Where had she met her husband-to-be, I wanted to know, trying to be patient despite the marked neglect of my concerns now that I had paid my money! Did she meet him through the agency? No. She'd placed a personal advertisement in a local magazine targeting her ethnic group. Hmm.

Next came "Brenda," yet another matchmaker who, in consultation with Barbara Baker, perused the files to find me a first match. They finally came up with "Irving." He had no college education, Brenda said, but he was the right religion, tall and nice-looking. He was "warm and caring"—characteristics used to describe every potential match, I soon learned.

Irving took some tracking down. Since his second divorce, he was living with his daughter in another county. After days of trying to contact him, Brenda decided he wasn't of "high enough quality" for me. She would look for someone else.

More than a week later, Brenda found "Cliff" in the files, another twice-divorced man, an artisan in business for himself. He was, of course, warm and caring, hard-working, and serious about marriage. Unfortunately, he too couldn't be contacted. I must be patient. He may be out of town. Yet another week passed before Brenda discovered that Cliff was in a serious relationship, although not with someone from Barbara Baker's Individual Search.

Brenda, still trying to find me a first match but getting noticeably desperate as she combed the files, suggested "Carl," a salesman, married fourteen years, divorced for twenty-five. "Why would I be interested in this man?" I asked, wondering what had happened to "the iceberg," the tip of which had yielded so many interesting and successful men. Brenda had no answer. Further, she had no file on Carl. "It's someone Barbara knows." Aha! Perhaps it was true about matchmakers calling on their brothers-in-law to fill the breach.

After meeting the first, decidedly ill-matched match, who was nothing like his profile, I called Brenda to complain. "Do you realize that lunch with that man cost me over $600 [one-sixth of the agency fee]? It wasn't worth it!"

Brenda suggested I visit the office for a more intensive discussion of what I was looking for. But now, I was to be handed over to "Kay," yet another matchmaker. Staff was constantly changing.

Kay—and Barbara Baker—together pulled files and discussed them with me. To my surprise, one was for "Rick," the man I had met months before through my personal advertisement in *The Nation*, the man who had been indignant that I was doing research for a book and who was happy to let me pay for my own lunch. I couldn't imagine he would have paid thousands of dollars for this kind of service.

"I've already met him." I told Kay, "So don't bother with that one." By coincidence, Rick called me a few days later, and I sounded out his experiences with the Barbara Baker agency.

Rick said the introductions he had received so far had not been interesting and the women no more well-matched than those he met through the personals at a fraction of the cost. He had indeed paid well for the services, even though he had negotiated the fee down to about half the asking price. Had he been more persistent, he need not have paid at all; I thought it kinder not to tell him that!

Caveat Emptor!

The six matches eventually dredged up for me by Barbara Baker's agency over a year or so—all described to me in ecstatic terms as "just right for you! This is the one for you; I feel it in my bones"—were ill-matched and some were wildly, even hilariously unsuitable! Religious beliefs, politics—we had hardly anything in common, except our growing fury with the Baker agency.

I learned at our first and only meeting that one of the men, a psychiatrist who had sounded as though he might be interesting, regularly consulted a psychic so he could see into his future! He didn't mention that during our initial telephone meeting, nor according to Kay, was it on his profile. Another's favorite pleasures were singing in karaoke bars and gambling in Las Vegas. These pursuits were not of the slightest interest to me. Yet another *loved* to shop! A generous and rich man, he spent all his leisure hours buying presents for his friends and family. I, on the other hand, *hate* shopping—and Kay knew this. If, when I die, I go to hell, I know it will be exactly like one of those giant malls!

The men and I kept asking each other "Did they even look at our profiles? What do they mean by "matching?" What it meant, I suspect, was that *any* male who was available was suggested in the agency's effort to provide the requisite number of "matches" my contract had stipulated. Each person I agreed to meet was counted, however unsuitable for me he turned out to be.

My experience with Barbara Baker's agency should encourage you to pause and consider before investing any money, let alone thousands of dollars, for the privilege of meeting a set number of matches. No doubt this particular organization has had some success in bringing together couples who ultimately marry. The percentage of those successes, though, is small, given the agency's own advertisements. It claimed to number over sixty thousand members in its singles organization and to have histories and background information on thirty-five hundred professional men and women. By contrast, the number of actual marriages listed was "more than 224" in one of their advertisements in 1996. (A figure of between three and four hundred was given in earlier advertisements.) Further, it is not clear from which membership pool these marriages were made.

We should be concerned, too, with the way male clients, particularly older men, are recruited. While fears that the proprietors use family members as matches may be unfounded, this agency and others do recruit men to boost their files of eligible partners. These men operate under private arrangements, meaning they don't pay for the service. One man told me he was a "personal friend" of Barbara Baker's; one was her accountant. Another man told me he served "as inventory" for this and other agencies.

Kay responded with indignation when I told her that one of her matches considered himself inventory. "I work hard to make *genuine* matches between serious people who are marriage-minded. Tell me which man said that to you, and we won't use him any more!"

I like Kay and I would like to believe her response was genuine, but my reservations about expensive matchmaking services remain.

Unexpected Complications

About Ladies First, the other matchmaking service I subscribed to, far less can be said than about Barbara Baker's Individual Search. Presenting themselves as "a matchmaking/dating service," the proprietors, "Philip" and "Mary," had organized dating projects such as singles mixers—dances and parties—before forming this new agency.

To keep costs low, Ladies First operated from Philip's oceanside apartment, the living room of which was converted into an efficient, comfortable office, equipped with computers, filing cabinets, and telephones. A glorious view of the Pacific filled the huge picture window.

The initial fee, to encourage enrollment, was $150 for a six-month membership, with full refund if a client changed her mind about joining within one month of signing.

"How can you afford to charge so little?" I wanted to know.

"Only by keeping overhead low and volume high. Neither of us draws a salary yet."

Both Philip and Mary knew I was researching the singles scene for a book (unlike Barbara Baker) and were eager to answer questions about their enterprise.

"To serve our women clients," they told me, "we have a pool, so far, of over one thousand men." It was from the *men* they derived most of their revenue. Men did not pay for membership, as did the women, but were charged a fee for each introduction. Both the men and the women regularly received a mailer of available matches of the opposite sex containing computerized photographs and brief printed descriptions.

Mary promised she would "check over everyone who comes in with you in mind and I'll call you as soon as I find someone suitable." She went on, "We'll look for someone really special for you." She crooned about my talents and "class" and looks. "You remind me of Deborah Kerr—such a lady! You deserve the best." Flattery is endemic, it seems, in this industry.

Several weeks passed without any word from Ladies First. I telephoned the office and was told by Philip that, as Mary's client, I should call her at her home. According to Mary, the organization was "re-forming." She and Philip had had a difference of opinion—to say the least. She was charging Philip with assault with a deadly weapon! He had tried, she insisted, to run down a friend of hers with his car, this assault being the last straw in a series of disagreements between the partners over the time each was investing in the service and how the business should be run.

Philip was continuing to operate Ladies First as a dating service, without the matchmaking component. Mary, shut out of Philip's apartment, could not reach her files so could not serve her clients. As far as I know, the partners' dispute remains to be resolved.

The old saying "You gets for what yer pays" may not apply to matchmakers. The expensive services are offered in fancy settings in fancy neighborhoods, but both expensive and inexpensive services may, or may not, deliver the desired results. The best a person can do is investigate several kinds of services and, as with any business transaction, read the fine print carefully before signing a contract.

BEFORE SIGNING WITH A MATCHMAKER . . .

§ Visit at least three agencies to compare costs and services.

§ Check the agencies with the Better Business Bureau or your state licensing board (or both) to discover past or pending legal actions.

§ Ask for referrals to satisfied clients. The response may be that clients are rarely willing to disclose this way of having met their spouses. Be persistent.

§ Ask how long the agency has been in business.

§ Ask how many marriages have resulted from the agency's efforts in the past year, in the past two years. Ask particularly about successful matches for people your age.

§ Ask how many men in your age range they have on their register.

§ Ask how they recruit men.

§ Ask how they investigate the men they have as clients.

§ Know exactly what the services will cost and what the services comprise.

§ Ask about methods of payment. Do they require all the money in advance of services, or can you pay in installments?

DANCES AND SOCIALS

Many people enjoy going to dances and socials, have a good time dancing with several partners, and meet compatible people there. I interviewed two women, one sixty-four and one sixty-seven, who met their current husbands at dances for fifty-plus singles, so this is a resource to consider. The bands are often good, playing the music of the 1940s and 1950s, as well as more contemporary dance tunes.

Most towns across the United States offer dances and mixers for singles and senior singles through churches and temples and senior centers. Some dances for the fifty-plus set are given in the afternoon on a Saturday or Sunday, so you need not worry about being out alone after dark. Call your local church or temple for information and watch your newspaper's guide to weekend activities for details.

Church and temple dances are usually relatively inexpensive—$5 or $6 for members, a couple of dollars more for visitors. Tickets are usually available at the door, and refreshments—coffee, tea, soft drinks, and nibbles—are often provided at reasonable prices. So you can sip on a soda while looking around to see who else has decided to attend.

Singles dances organized by private entrepreneurs will be more expensive. Besides ballroom dancing, square dances and folk dances also seem to attract older patrons and provide good opportunities for people to meet.

Most advisors to single people suggest women go alone to dances and other functions as men are, supposedly, a bit hesitant about approaching two or more women chatting together. I *did* go alone to a dance but soon fell into conversation with women at my table. As a researcher looking for information, I always talk to people wherever I am. This did not appear to deter the men, as each of us women in the group had many partners and danced almost every dance. Functions listed for singles of any age are clearly intended to help men and women meet each other, and everyone knows this.

Nowadays, there is nothing to prevent a woman from asking a man to dance, and many sets are designated "Ladies' Choice." You may have to summon up your courage if you are shy, but approaching a prospective dance partner gets easier with practice. Men tell me *they* often find it difficult to approach a woman for a dance as the women are not always tactful. One man's request for a turn around the floor was dismissed with "You're not my type!" The man came back with "I'm asking for a dance, not to *marry* you!"

Once on the floor with a partner, you have the chance to learn a little bit about the man—and to smile at him fetchingly, if that's how you feel!

SINGLES ORGANIZATIONS

Increasingly, the needs of single people are being catered to by for-profit as well as nonprofit organizations. Mixers, conversation evenings, and other events are held in most communities, many of them advertised in the local media.

The majority of these events are held for younger people, but some organizations, such as Parents Without Partners, welcome people of any age. So even if your children are grown up and long gone, you are eligible. Other events are arranged for the over-forty and the fifty-plus sets.

Most local newspapers publish a directory of singles events on a specific day of the week. It appears in my paper on Fridays. The most recent issue lists, among others happenings:

§ "The Tennis Players: Meet, Play, Travel, 40 plus."

§ "Singles 50-plus dance, including line-dance lessons."

§ "Social Gathering for Single Believers."

§ "Singles Parties, 15 men, 15 women. Different parties for different age groups. Dinner. Dancing aboard boat."

§ "A Night on Broadway: Show tunes party with singers. Sing-along. . . ."

§ "The Big Difference. Party for Big Beautiful People.

§ "Golf Fore Singles: N/S men and women. Dinner after."

§ "Singles Walk. All ages."

§ "Gourmet Dining Adventures for Singles."

§ "Good Conversation and Delicious Dessert. 40 plus"

In the newspaper you will also find listings for church and temple singles organizations that hold a variety of events, including mixers, for all age groups. Even if you haven't attended services for years, make a call. You'll be welcomed. You may also be recruited to help organize a party, or a dance, or a concert yourself!

I did attend a number of singles conversation evenings, some for mixed ages and some for the fifty-plus crowd. These can be enjoyable if you find a compatible group and if the topics interest you. Usually, there's a charge of ten dollars and up, which includes refreshments and soft drinks.

Many of these gatherings, certainly in California, are run by therapists and psychologists with various backgrounds as a kind of addition to their regular practices, and they are often as much a way for people to vent their feelings about their pain, loneliness, and unhappiness in a nonthreatening situation as they are to meet members of the opposite sex.

People often talk freely about their personal experiences, their hurts and disappointments, and their hopes for meeting the right person. At some of these events, you may find the conversation too confessional. Other evenings may provide fascinating discussions in which you learn a lot about different ways of living. As in any group of single people, you may make new friends—of either sex—or you may meet a man you like enough to arrange to meet in another setting.

Nonprofit singles groups for the fifty-plus crowd also hold conversation evenings in private homes, among other activities such as bowling and trips to the museum and theater outings. The range of topics is considerable. It can include financial management; travels to exotic locations; relationships with adult children; understanding the stock market; and so on.

At one I attended, the speaker dealt specifically with finding suitable partners, so I listened carefully and took notes! When I looked up from my note pad, I was amused to notice that the group members, roughly equal numbers of men and women, were less interested in what the speaker had to say than in stealing glances at each other! During the break for refreshments and at the end of the evening, there was considerable exchanging of cards and phone numbers and arranging of future dates!

Travel clubs provide another way to meet members of the opposite sex. Travel agents should be able to help you find an ocean or river cruise or a foreign travel plan for groups of mature singles. Look through your AARP (American

Association for Retired Persons) magazines and newsletters too for information about travel for single people.

If you are an outdoors type, you might want to look into the Sierra Club. This organization is concerned with the environment and with conserving the natural wonders of the earth. It, too, has its singles groups: Sierra Club Singles offers fun and outdoors activities specifically for single people in a range of age groups.

As you begin looking into one or more of these possibilities, you will discover more opportunities than you could have imagined for single people to meet other single people in your area. A few telephone calls will perhaps lead you to umbrella organizations in your area that publish details of every singles event for miles around and, for a small membership fee, regularly mail out their own magazines. Listings in these publications are often arranged by categories such as religion, age, specialized interests, workshops, and so on. Take a good look at the "Bulletin Board" and "Listings" sections of your local newspapers, both the regular newspapers and the free news sheets, for singles events that might interest you. You may be surprised at what you find!

In this chapter and the previous one, we looked at a range of *direct* ways to meet members of the opposite sex: through personal advertisements in newspapers and magazines; by organizing your own singles events; through on-line services; by going to dances and socials; by using dating and matchmaking services; and by attending events presented by for-profit and nonprofit organizations. Now we'll turn to other, less direct, resources.

Chapter Five

Enriching Your Life While Looking for Love

Medical researchers and other scientists are increasingly finding what most of us have long known—that keeping active, intellectually and socially as well as physically, is good for you! "Use it or lose it" applies to one's mental acuity and one's social skills as well as to one's libido! Further, experts in gerontology make a clear distinction between passive aging and successful aging. To engage in successful aging involves a conscious commitment to continuing self-education, both for its own sake and for the sake of one's well-being.

Only 10 percent of Americans sixty-five and over have a chronic health problem that restricts them from major physical activity. Some of the rest of us, including those still many years from sixty-five, may need a little push to reap the benefits of getting out of the house, enriching our lives, becoming involved in some pleasurable activity—and perhaps finding love in the process.

Even if you don't feel ready for the more direct ways of looking for love, consider the list of possible life-enriching activities I have gathered for you here. Choose something that interests you and follow through! At the same time, let yourself approach—and be open to—possible new friendships.

Draw on your new-found courage, and introduce yourself to that man in the group who is without a partner and who might be pleasant company. If there's a man sitting alone along the row at a concert, or studying the same painting at the museum, smile and say hello. What can it hurt? If you are out in the world, alive and alert, there is no end of ordinary ways to bump into people, start a conversation, go for coffee and. . . . This is the stuff of stories in romance magazines; it's also the stuff of real life: men and women chat over the water cooler at work; their shopping carts get entangled in the supermarket; they watch their laundry going around together at the Laundromat; or, as happened to me, they meet while doing their regular stint of jogging or walking.

For eighteen years or so, since we moved into the house I still live in, I have walked the four miles around the reservoir near my home four or five times a week. As a well-married woman, I was only dimly aware of "The Lake" as a place to meet members of the opposite sex, and more recently, although I had seen "Terry" running with a small group of other men, I had not noticed him. He, it seems, had noticed me, and one day, he left his group and walked and talked by my side. He talked a good talk, and I was pleased when, a week or so later, he invited me out to dinner.

If you stay home, you'll meet no one but the person who reads the gas meter. When you are involved in something you like, you will almost certainly meet new people and make friends—of both sexes. Yes, it may turn out that the man you spoke to might not be friendly—or single—but the next one might be. Meantime, you are doing something you enjoy.

The world is rich with marvelous opportunities for realizing your talents, for expanding your horizons, for making new friends, for bringing enchantment. This is *your* time!

CHURCHES, TEMPLES, AND OTHER RELIGIOUS OR SPIRITUAL ORGANIZATIONS

Churches and temples offer a wide range of social and socially conscious activities that may provide outlets for your "giving" side. But hardly any giving is entirely altruistic. "Give and you shall receive."

Within one week, a church and a temple in my neighborhood put on a Civil War Band Concert; a comedy night, the proceeds going to a foodbank; a hilarious set of "readings"—some by professional stand-up comedians—of the biblical story of Esther; a pot-luck supper for singles; and a bridge night.

You may find congenial friends and a sense of community at the church or temple you were associated with as a child, or if you feel more spiritual than religious, you may be comfortable with the Unitarians or some similarly "accepting" and nondoctrinaire church. The religious services directory in the Saturday issue of my city's newspaper lists sixty-two denominations with more than three hundred places of worship or spiritual awareness. And by no means does the paper list all such services available in the area. In some cities, there are more churches than there are pubs in London!

If you are already a churchgoer, you know that many churches provide all kinds of services to the community. You may find a cause that appeals to your philosophy and that satisfies a personal need to be of service while being among like-minded people. This need not be the more obvious kind of "doing good" but may involve putting on orchestral or choral concerts, organizing festivals, or helping with celebrations. People are always needed to advertise, to sell tickets, and to encourage gift-giving and raise money. You will be welcomed if you bring any of these skills or even if you just bring your willing self. You can be sure they'll find something for you to do!

Churches and temples also offer courses and group discussions on topics both religious and secular that you might enjoy. If you would like to have some influence on the direction your church will take in the future, perhaps you could consider serving as an active board member or on a committee that will debate an issue you care about.

Think about it. If it has any appeal, try it!

MUSEUMS AND OTHER CULTURAL INSTITUTIONS

Most cities boast at least one museum; large cities offer several. As a member of the Los Angeles County Museum of Art, I can speak at first hand about some of the activities I have enjoyed recently.

Museums do not just house their own, often excellent, permanent holdings of paintings and other works, they also host visiting exhibits from the world's finest collections. In recent months, my museum offered splendid, docent-led tours of a Kandinsky exhibit, an exhibit entitled "Picasso's Women," and a collection of previously hidden paintings by Gustave Caillebotte, the French Impressionist, among other special showings of photographs and glass and china.

Even if you know quite a lot about art and are already enjoying your main museum's offerings, why not look around for galleries that specialize in, say, modern art or miniature art or antique dolls or Americana or classic cars or some other form of art that might be new to you.

I am constantly astonished at the range of museums in many American cities: museums of natural history; Jewish museums; children's museums (My daughter and I, both grown-ups, had a wonderful day of play at the Children's Museum in Indianapolis one afternoon!); museums dealing with movies, radio, and television; aeronautics museums. The list varies from city to city, so look in your newspaper's listings of museums or in the Yellow Pages for what is available near you.

Moreover, many museums make available other offerings in addition to exhibits, including:

§ Silent movie programs

§ Modern film classics programs

§ Concerts, jazz as well as classical—some city museums offer summer season outdoor concerts

§ Lecture series and talks on art and art history

§ Hands-on art classes

§ Access to research libraries

§ Occasional parties or exhibit previews for members

If art is one of your passions, you may consider becoming a

docent yourself. This will take time, first for training and then to lead tours, but you will learn more about art than you could have imagined, meet hundreds of people, and make friends with interests similar to your own. At the time of this writing, my city's Museum of Contemporary Art advertised in the local newspaper for volunteers: "No special skills are needed, only an interest in contemporary art and the desire to learn more about the artists who shape contemporary culture. Volunteers help staff the information desk, aid museum staff at special events, and provide general office and project assistance."

The museum in your town may have just such a place for you, or you might offer to become a "friend" of the museum before making heavy commitments.

Other cultural institutions, besides museums, include zoological gardens, botanical gardens, and aquariums. They, too, may hold classes and offer opportunities to participate more directly than simply as a ticket-holding visitor. Again, let your local newspaper and the Yellow Pages guide you to activities that interest you or that might broaden your horizons.

POLITICAL ORGANIZATIONS

Politics touches all our lives. It is about power at every level. It has to do with the price of a loaf of bread or a head of lettuce as well as with who wins the next election or which groups are doing battle with which other groups.

If you want to get involved in the decisions made in your community or in the nation—decisions about social security or about civil rights, decisions about local schools or about amending the Constitution—go to it!

You may choose to work with your local Democratic, Republican, or other party, or you may prefer nonpartisan politics or grassroots activism.

Are you furious that your street is no longer swept by the local authority? Do you feel keenly that too little is being done for children before and after school? Are you concerned that some programs for poor people are being undermined? Only you know the issues that excite you or make you angry.

Read your local newspapers, including the "underground" sheets or the "free" presses, for community concerns. Follow up with telephone calls, either directly to the newspaper or to the reporter or writer or to anyone involved in the issue. Find out where the matter is being discussed, what is being planned, who is leading the campaign, how you might play a part.

More conventionally, telephone the local office of your representative in Congress or in the Senate, or in your state legislature. Call someone on the city council or the county board of supervisors. Find out what is going on, when votes are to be taken, what the arguments are for and against, so you can make informed decisions.

Groups form around important issues. People involved in politics are passionate. They care about outcomes. They'll welcome your participation, draw you into the fold, and take all your time and energy, if you allow it. That's up to you.

VOLUNTEERING: DOING WELL WHILE DOING GOOD!

Many of the nonprofit helping organizations, such as The American Red Cross, the American Cancer Society, Catholic Charities, The Salvation Army, and so on, would not be able to provide services to those in need without their dedicated volunteers. The teams of trained people dispatched by the Red Cross after a fire or an earthquake are volunteers. The people who offer information and advice at health fairs are volunteers. The men and women who travel across the country to be of service to victims of floods or hurricanes, setting up shelters, helping people get their lives back together, are volunteers. The men and women who research, write, and publish these organizations' newsletters are volunteers. The people who go out into the community to talk to groups about what to do before, during, and after a disaster are volunteers.

In many city newspapers, an "Involvement Opportunities" column may point you towards other ways of volunteering your time that will both interest you and bring you in touch with like-minded people. Your help may be needed at the local animal shelter or at the hospital, for instance. Another route is to find your nearest

chapter of Volunteers of America or a similar umbrella organization. A telephone call will inform you of numerous helping organizations needing volunteers that you may choose among.

The rewards for helping others really can't be measured.
You experience a genuine feeling of self-worth, of real useful-
ness. Further, a sense of comradeship develops between the
members of these organizations, especially when they have
worked together more than once as part of a team, traveled
together to a disaster site, shared some of the same experiences.
This comradeship can, and often does, develop into more than
affection. Volunteers can be of any age group, but retired people
often have more time to be of service than younger people.
You'll find lots of active, caring "silver foxes," men as well as
women, among the ranks of volunteers.

DISCUSSION AND CONVERSATION GROUPS

In recent years, the salon movement, if it can be called that, has
grown. Some of us love to *talk*! We miss ordinary talk if we live
alone—"How was your day?" We miss worldly, trade, and intellectual talk if we no longer go out to work. "Salons," something
like the artists' and writers' groups of the past, are appearing all
over the country. They were written about some years ago in *The
Utne Reader*, an alternative press magazine that reprints articles
from less-known periodicals than those regularly appearing on
the newsstands. Readers can subscribe to a newsletter, separate
from the magazine, that updates information about salons in
various parts of the country.

Salons come and go; there may, or may not, be some in your
neighborhood, but you can certainly start one of your own
around topics you care about. My friend "Joy," who lives in a
semirural area, recently began a salon at her home. Salons are
usually held in private homes. In some cases people meet regularly at one address. Other groups rotate the meeting place from
home to home each month, the host providing refreshments.

How do you find people to attend your salon? You can see
what's in the personals in your local newspaper or advertise
yourself, taking the same precautions as you would if you were

seeking suitable companionship of the opposite sex (see Chapters 2 and 6). Many newspapers provide a "Mutual Interests" section. Screen the callers, call them back, and talk at length before giving your address or phone number to anyone. For safety's sake, let a close friend or family member know what you are doing, or better yet, have that person on hand, at least for the first meeting.

How would you organize your salon? Joy, who loves to read, asked members to select a short passage from a book that they either loved or that had been influential in their lives. They were to be prepared to read the passage aloud to the group and to say why they had chosen it. The group had to be small enough for everyone to have his or her say and large enough for a varied sampling of tastes and points of view. A leader is usually elected—perhaps a different person at each meeting—to make sure that people stay focused on the topic. During the break or after the formal discussion, the participants can enjoy some purely social time together.

At the end of some salons, members are given a copy of a magazine or journal article to read and prepare for discussion at the next gathering. The articles may concern some aspect of the economy or changing relationships between the sexes or any other subject that interests the group. At other salons a film or a documentary is shown and people bring their opinions and experience to enliven the discussion that follows. Salon topics are as varied as the groups who participate in them.

Along similar lines, book clubs are also popular. Usually, one book is chosen for discussion. Then everyone reads the book and brings comments to the meeting. If the group agrees, one member may be chosen to do research each month—find published reviews of the book to present *after* everyone has delivered his or her feelings about the work.

Established book clubs prepare their list of books for an entire year, decide where each monthly meeting will be held, and determine who will prepare the buffet for that evening. Not only do you read books carefully and with purpose, but you also go into other people's homes and see how they live and entertain! When it's your turn as host, you can knock your guests' socks off with your chocolate cake or your roasted eggplant!

Many bookstores have bulletin boards where people who wish to start or join book groups may post notices. Also, book clubs exist within other organizations—churches, for example. Publishers now also publish book club guides.

Know, too, that many of the large chain bookstores, such as Barnes and Noble, Bookstar, and Borders, as well as the smaller booksellers, are increasingly becoming social centers of a sort. People who enjoy a wide range of interests can come and browse, listen to instructive lectures, drink coffee, meet old friends, and make new friends—as well as buy a book, magazine, or newspaper. Many of the bookstores stay open well into the evening, some until midnight.

As I mentioned in Chapter 4, conversation groups and chat clubs are increasingly widespread now on the Internet. If you are computer-literate and have an on-line service, you can meet people in cyberspace—and you can meet them in person, after you have learned about them on the screen. Again, the same precautions apply as when meeting strangers through the personals or any other way.

Conversation clubs can be formed around a wide range of interests including politics, art, cooking, or any of hundreds of hobbies.

HOBBIES: COLLECTING, ARTS AND CRAFTS, PAINTING, AND SO ON

Take a trip to your local newsstand or library, and see the number of magazines devoted to individual and specialized interests. Do you think no one but you cares about collecting antique toys? or comic books? or teddy bears? or teapots? You'll be astonished at how many people have the same tastes as you, so many that probably there is a magazine, or several magazines, devoted to informing followers about latest trends, clubs, meetings. Other people have the same fancies as you. Now is the time to follow that fancy!

If you love arts and crafts but haven't investigated the possibilities, a whole world of artsy-craftsy activities awaits you! People who enjoy working with their hands—throwing pots on a wheel, carving wooden wildfowl, making rugs, framing pictures, taking photographs, building models, designing textiles or jewelry—are eager to share their interests. Arts and crafts fairs are held all over the country. If the magazines are expensive, you may be able to read them at your public library.

Have you checked out the offerings at your local community college? Would you like to try your hand at slab pottery? See what classes are lined up for next term. Have you envied those people in that group on the river bank painting the old mill or sketching the boats on the water? Ask how you can join them, or a similar group. You've always felt you have some talent as a cartoonist, or a writer, or a poet, but you were too busy to develop your artistic side. Now is the time to go ahead, get some guidance, and meet other budding artists.

Specialized magazines, of which there are hundreds, perhaps thousands, give the latest trends and provide diaries of forthcoming events you might be able to attend. A look in your local bookstore is almost sure to reveal something of interest to you. The inset on page 97 will provide you with just a sample of the many specialized magazines that are available.

MUSIC AND THEATER

Many of us are music or theater lovers, true supporters of these arts, even though we may not play an instrument or act or sing. Nowadays, we can listen to the world's greatest composers on records, audiotapes, or compact discs and see the finest dramas on television or by renting videos. These feed our souls, and we can enjoy them alone as well as among crowds.

Consider, though, becoming *personally* involved in music-making or theatrical production, not as an artist but as support. The community theater in your town or nearby may be struggling to stay alive. It depends on people like you to volunteer for some of the administrative and practical tasks that help keep the doors open. All small theaters have to raise money. Can you help with the intermission buffet? Can you show people to their seats? Can you help design costumes, build scenery, set up lighting or props, put up posters, man (or woman) the box office, place advertisements in local businesses? Not only will you be helping the theater, you will also be among actors and stage

SPECIALIZED MAGAZINES

This partial list will give you taste of the variety available.

American Collector	*Lapidary Journal*
Audubon	*Modern Railway Journal*
Bicycling	*Natural History*
Birders World	*Photo Techniques*
Bridge Magazine	*Poets and Writers*
Cat Fancy	*Popular Photography*
Chess Life	*Postcard Collector*
Climbing	*Quilt*
Contemporary Doll	*Sculpture Review*
Collector	*Southwest Art*
Disneyana	*Spin-off* (a magazine
(for collectors)	for spinners)
Dog World	*Teddy Bear*
Doll Reader	*Weavers*
Field and Stream	*WildBird*
Fine Woodworking	*Writer's Digest*

people, professional or amateur, talking about theater, watching rehearsals, going out for coffee with the cast and crew, *enjoying yourself!*

Large city orchestras also rely on their "friends"—volunteers who love music and want it to thrive—for fund-raising events, for encouraging new subscribers, for producing newsletters, and for selling souvenirs. The chamber orchestra in my town has an outreach program that presents several short concerts each year in junior high schools and high schools. Preparing students to appreciate the music involves having docents (guides) go into classrooms to talk about the music the young people will be hearing.

The docents might not be musicians themselves, nor might they be able to read music. So they are given a little training and some tapes and other tools to take with them. Docents attend the school concerts, of course, and are invited to several brunches and other events, including concerts in the regular series. Make a few phone calls, and see how you might fit into a group of interested and interesting supporters or a backstage team.

Large organizations depending heavily on community support try to treat their volunteers with a great deal of respect, putting on award luncheons and banquets and other activities to encourage continuing participation and to ensure that volunteers know how valuable they are. Participants are made to feel part of a caring family. Smaller groups, struggling for survival, also cherish their volunteers and make much of them. You can be part of that.

If you do play a musical instrument, or if you *used* to play but haven't sung a note or touched the piano or the trumpet for years, this may be the time to get back into playing. Brush up your skills and join a band, orchestra, glee club, or choir. Your local community college or university music department has a place for you, even if you don't play like Wynton Marsalis or sing like Cecilia Bartoli! Hardly anyone else does, either. You may not be playing Carnegie Hall any time soon, but you'll be having fun.

DANCING

Social dancing can be a good way to meet members of the opposite sex. However, if you like dancing but feel too pressured to find a partner at social dances, there are many other dancing opportunities to explore.

Line-dancing, folk dancing, flamenco, and square dancing do not require couples. You can go alone and know you'll have lots of strenuous fun. Again, your community college may offer Middle Eastern or Greek or Armenian or Polish or Irish dance classes or a combination of several kinds of ethnic dancing for beginners and for those with more experience. Enthusiasts who take these classes, and instructors who teach them, know where and when ethnic dances are held in public places—restaurants, perhaps, and clubs and church halls. You love to dance? Why are you waiting?

SPORTS, FITNESS, OUTDOOR ACTIVITIES

Physical activity will keep you fit. If you haven't got that message yet, you haven't been listening! Every doctor who writes in popular magazines or talks on television or sees you in his office is telling you to get out there and walk or play tennis or swim or cycle—after you've made sure you are ready for it. Walking and jogging and other physical pursuits not only help us to keep in shape and perhaps live longer, but they are also enjoyable ways of meeting people and expanding our social circle.

While the lone walker or hiker, runner or jogger, may get only nods from passers-by, the member of a hiking or cycling or sports club will have access to many club activities. These may include socials, dances, talks, and perhaps slide or photograph exhibits by those who walk or hike across the United States and in foreign countries, making friends all over the world.

The Sierra Club and other organizations that promote the well-being of the environment offer walkers, climbers, skiers, and other nature lovers activities to participants at all levels of expertise from beginner to very experienced. These outings and events can take place in cities, in suburbs, in the local mountains, out of your state, and abroad. They include nature workshops, mountaineering, white-water rafting, simple walks in your neighborhood. You can also become involved in pending legislation to stop speculators from building in your local mountains, or to clean your polluted lake. If you can't find the address of your local chapter of the Sierra Club, write to headquarters at Sierra Club, 85 Second Street, San Francisco, CA 94105-3441.

Have you thought about learning golf? Or if you know how to play but haven't been on a course for a long time, why not get back into it? It's a wonderful way to spend a few hours in the open air. Tennis too, although a more strenuous activity, is a great way to get out of the house and to meet other people who enjoy the sport. Many city parks offer relatively inexpensive access to these and other sports activities.

To simply get and stay in shape, keep-fit classes are everywhere. Again, look to the community college. Senior citizen's centers have keep-fit classes, as well as other activities. The health club is also an option, including the YMCA, where membership fees may be lower than at commercial clubs, if you'd like access to the kinds of exercise equipment and weight machines few of us can have at home. Many health clubs also have swimming pools and hot tubs as well as organized classes led by professional fitness instructors.

Other sports activities might include walking, running, bowling in a league, swimming, backpacking, yoga, martial arts, fishing, hunting, boating, and many more, depending on your tastes and energy level. You could train for and join in one of the many walkathons for charity. These activities are often listed in the "Calendar" section of the local newspaper. You can also call the YMCA or YWCA, the senior center, or the bowling lanes, or even drop in at one of the specialized sporting goods shops for information and flyers that advertise forthcoming events or newly forming groups. Your city or country recreation department will also be able to advise you of organized and supervised sports activities and places in your areas where you might swim or play tennis.

TRAVEL AND ADVENTURE

You always said that when you had time or were free or could afford it, you would travel. Most of us view travel in rather general terms. Perhaps we think of Paris and London and Prague—the world's great cities—and envisage ourselves, usually in the company of some vague "other," dashing carefree from concert, to museum, to theater, "having a wonderful time," as people always seem to say on their postcards from exotic places.

You never visualized yourself traveling alone, and you don't fancy it much. Where's the fun if you can't share the new and wonderful experiences with someone close?

Now perhaps you *will* find a friend willing and able to take a trip with you, and you'll both have good times and great memories together. If no friend is available, though, you need not sit at home, growing ever greener with envy at the stories told by people venturing—and adventuring—all over the globe.

You can go it alone, and you may find that traveling alone has some advantages over being with someone else: You can come and go as you please; you can eat when and where you fancy; you can go to a museum or visit a cathedral, or you can spend the day reading in the park without having to explain yourself; you can go at your own pace—not necessarily slowly.

Among my most adventurous acquaintances is "Meg," a woman in her mid-sixties who, for the past eighteen years has been on the road to many parts of the world, particularly Southeast Asia, Alaska, and "anyplace where there are mountains."

She had dreamed of climbing mountains ever since she was a child. Her parents subscribed to *National Geographic*, which she would read from cover to cover. Fascinated by the stories of Sir Edmund Hillary and other such travelers, she longed for the same kinds of adventures.

Meg has done much of her traveling alone. "I wanted to go to places where my friends didn't want to go, and I decided not to wait for someone to go with."

As a lone woman traveler, she provides both inspiration and good, solid, practical tips for other women who may be thinking about setting off alone but are uncertain how to go about it and whether they will enjoy it.

"On your own, you are more likely to meet new people than if you are one of a couple or of a group. People are less likely to feel they are intruding, and they'll talk to you."

A successful trip depends on careful planning and preparation. "Do background checking," Meg says. "Know the culture and what you need to do to fit in. Ask yourself why you might want to go to, say, Indonesia. To study the art? the crafts? What do you want to see and experience? What is appropriate clothing? Know about the people and their lives. You'll be respected for it."

As an example of how she sets up a solo trip, Meg tells of her travels in Borneo a few years ago. She had read an article about Gunung Mulu National Park, the largest national park in Malaysia, over a million and a quarter acres, in the Malaysian part of Borneo. For the three-day inland journey on the water, she would have to take a variety of water crafts: high-speed boats, then long boats, then river canoes. In Borneo, the rivers are the roadways.

Once she knew where she wanted to go, Meg made the arrangements through a travel agent. Within the park, she was provided with a guide—an absolute necessity—and a porter, both Borneo tribesmen. She was then taken to the most extensive caves in the world, the prehistoric caves that were home to the early cave dwellers. Her stay outside the park was in a mixture of hotels and camps.

Your first trip alone doesn't have to be to the interior of Borneo! Meg has been traveling alone for a long time, one major trip each year during her vacation time from her job as an administrator for a nonprofit organization. But why shouldn't you, too, plan an exciting adventure to a place of your choice? Meg says she has made friends all over the world, writes to them regularly, and often goes to stay with them and has them visit her.

If I've whetted your appetite for solo travel, you might like to read one or more of the books listed in the inset on page 103. You will learn everything you need to know before setting off on travels both within the United States and abroad, including journeying to some really exotic and unusual locales.

SENIOR CITIZENS' GROUPS, RSVP, AARP, ELDERHOSTEL

Many of us do not like to think of ourselves as "seniors." I loathe that term myself. Intensely. Remember, though, that for some purposes, people of fifty years old are considered seniors, and many organizations for this age group offer all kinds of opportunities for relatively inexpensive individual and group travel, classes, social events, and occasions for having a good time.

RSVP gets people involved in providing services and working on local issues specifically for and about older people. To find a group in your area, look in the government pages in your telephone book under "Senior Citizens."

The American Association for Retired Persons (AARP) produces an excellent monthly magazine, *Modern Maturity*, with informative, entertaining, and inspiring articles and ideas about

TRAVEL BOOKS

Natania Jansz and Miranda Davies, editors, *More Women Travel*, Tough Guides, 1995. (Write to 375 Hudson Street, 3rd floor, New York, NY 10014.)

Sally M. Maisel, *Cruising Solo: The Single Traveler's Guide to Adventure on the High Seas*, Marin Publications, 1993. (Write to 4 Highland Avenue, San Rafael, CA 94901, or call 415-459-3817.)

Maggie and Gemma Moss, *Handbook for Women Travelers*, Piatkus, 1995. (Write to 5 Windmill Street, London W1, England.)

Sharon B. Wingler, *Travel Alone and Love It*, Chicago Spectrum Press, 1996. (Write to 1572 Sherman Avenue, Annex C, Evanston, IL 60201, or call 800-594-5190.)

Thalia Zepatos, *A Journey of One's Own*, The Eighth Mountain Press, 1996. (Write to 624 Southeast 29th Avenue, Portland, OR 97214, or call 503-233-3936.)

engaging yourself in the world. Anyone fifty years old and older may join; membership in AARP costs only a few dollars a year. Flashing your card may win you substantial discounts, particularly in hotels and motels and for renting cars. For details write to AARP, 3200 East Carson Street, Lakewood, CA 90712.

Elderhostel is a nonprofit educational organization offering short-term academic programs at educational institutions—college campuses, for example—both in the United States and all over the world. People sixty years of age and older are eligible (a spouse may accompany a participant if he or she is at least fifty years old). You can read the classics at an American university, study art in Rome and Florence, learn about history in Spain. You can cycle in Great Britain or Denmark or Austria or France or the Netherlands, study Aboriginal heritage and culture in Australia and on and on, all without ever taking an exam! Accommodations are usually in college and university dormitories, not necessarily fancy—but friendly!

Elderhostel also offers service programs for people fifty-five and over. These allow you to do valuable work at the same time as you travel to new places, meet new people, and make new friends. It is also possible that some of the costs of these programs can count as deductibles against your income taxes. Service programs include volunteering at Habitat for Humanity, a Christian ministry that works in many parts of the world, as well as in the United States, helping to provide decent housing, literacy classes, and other services for poor and homeless people. Other service programs provide volunteers for work in museums, or for historical societies, or archaeology projects, or saving the whales—and much more. For information about these and any of the Elderhostel programs, write to Elderhostel, 75 Federal Street, Boston, MA 02110-1941.

Road Scholar tours, by Saga Holidays, a commercial company, are for people of fifty and over. Groups go to many parts of the United States and abroad and are treated to lectures and visits to places of interest guided by experts. Saga charges extra for single people, and accommodations are usually good hotels with private bathrooms. You can send for a brochure to Saga International Holidays, Ltd., 222 Berkeley Street, Boston, MA 02116. Or call 1-800-621-2151.

CLASSES, EDUCATION, TEACHING

You can study almost any subject in the world! What interests you? Apart from all the academic subjects, like history and philosophy, literature and psychology, music or art appreciation, you will find classes in yoga, human relationships, desktop publishing, computer applications, the stock market, managing your money, alternative medicine, massage, how to play chess, understanding plumbing, interior decorating, bread baking, and so on. Attending every one of those classes are people like you, interested in knowing more about an intriguing topic and perhaps as eager as you to meet new people and develop friendships. Some courses, such as automobile maintenance and repair, attract more men than women—and didn't you need to know more about your car, anyway?

If you have a flair for teaching, even though you may not have teaching credentials you may be able to train to help new-comers adapt to American culture, or you might choose to work with people who cannot read or write, Americans as well as people from abroad. Teaching English as a second language can be both enjoyable and fulfilling, as can teaching reading to chil-dren, young people, or adults. Literacy programs are often given through public libraries or through adult education. A phone call to your local library should give you a start.

ETHNIC GROUP INTERESTS

Everyone who lives in the United States, unless he or she is a Native American, has either come here from somewhere else or is descended from immigrants.

The United States was once thought to be a melting pot in which people from all over the world would forget their pasts and become, simply, Americans. It sometimes seems, though, that someone forgot to light the fire under that pot and that America is a mixed salad, rather than a stew, each vegetable clearly separate from the others.

Not everyone approves of the trend, but in recent years we have seen the "hyphenation of America." People refer to them-selves as Polish-American, Mexican-American, African-American, Irish-American, and so on. People of various ethnic heritages take pride in discovering, or rediscovering, their roots, planning group visits back to the old country, at the same time that they remain solidly American.

Perhaps in your area, your ethnic group is prominent, with easy-to-find places of worship and clubs with activities for peo-ple of all ages. Or perhaps you may have to search out ethnic group organizations, but the effort can prove rewarding. The search can begin with the telephone book. You can also place one of those free or low-cost notices in the "Mutual Interests" section of the newspaper.

CLUBS

Just as people get together for conversation, so they gather to combine their knowledge and to do more than simply talk and philosophize. Among the clubs you might consider joining—or starting—are investment clubs, where members research bull and bear markets, mutual funds, stock options, commodities, junk bonds, penny stocks, and so on. Some groups regularly pool and invest modest sums, evidently doing quite well financially.

Other clubs center around playing bridge or other card games, or chess or Scrabble or any of several board games. These are not gambling clubs; they are noncommercial, players meeting in private homes. Occasionally, you will find advertisements in the "Mutual Interests" section of the personals pages for people to join such a group. Or you could advertise yourself.

GO TO IT!

The opportunities for you to reach out and become involved in absorbing and enjoyable activities, to keep on learning and growing, to do some good at the same time as you make new friends and, perhaps, find love are all around you. All you have to do is seize them.

They say that you can lead a horse to the water, but you can't make him drink—unless he wants to and is ready.

You are ready!

Chapter Six

Taking a Chance on Love

Whenever I mention the kinds of personal research I have conducted for this book—advertising in magazines and newspapers; answering personal ads; driving to dances or other functions alone; going out to meet a man known only through a letter or a telephone conversation; chatting to a fellow hiker on a morning walk—someone always draws in his or her breath and protests: "But that's so *dangerous*! You never know who these people are. You are taking terrible chances!"

The vision of the ax murderer or the serial killer looms large, and many women, and some men, become so immobilized by their fear of what lurks outside their door, they refuse to go out at all. They remain virtual prisoners of their own imaginings. You will not be one of those people because you will be well prepared to look after yourself!

We *do* live in a dangerous society; we could be gunned down in the streets in any of our cities at any time. Newspapers and news broadcasts overwhelm us with stories of purse snatchings and knifings on buses, apartment break-ins, stabbings at the automated teller machines, muggings, even in lighted areas. Occasionally, things do fall out of the sky! And more

Americans are killed on our roads each year than were killed in the entire Vietnam War.

Some of life's dangers are beyond our control, but we can protect ourselves against others. We have to first identify possible dangers and then decide what can be done to avoid or reduce the risks. If the situation looks as though it's beyond our control, we can then decide not to take that particular chance. If we can see ways of protecting ourselves, we can be a bit daring.

Possible risks for older women and men entering, or re-entering, the world of dating and mating include the physical, the financial, and the emotional.

PROTECTING YOURSELF AGAINST PHYSICAL RISKS

You know this stuff already: You probably said these things to your children, again and again. They can't be said too often, however.

§ Don't give your address to strangers.

§ Meet in a public place until you develop trust.

§ Use your own transportation.

§ Carry some cash or credit cards.

§ Carry change for the telephone.

§ Take a course in self-defense.

§ Take precautions against sexually transmitted diseases.

Never invite strangers to your home until they are no longer strangers! This means you don't give your address to anyone until you feel reasonably sure he won't hurt you when you are alone with him, or try to break into your house to carry off your precious possessions when you aren't at home.

You'll notice that when you are ready to leave a message, either for people answering your personal advertisement or when you are answering someone else's, you"ll be instructed, for your protection, not to give your surname and to give only the name of your neighborhood and not your full address. It's only common sense.

When you meet a member of the opposite sex for the first time, arrange to meet in the daytime, in a public place with other people around. Disaster-preparedness training, such as earthquake readiness, stresses always having at least a quarter of a tank of gas in your car. You don't want anything to prevent you from making a quick getaway, if you need to.

Make sure you have some cash and a credit card so you can get home or make an emergency telephone call. It's also a good idea to tell someone you trust where you are going and roughly the time you expect to return home.

Don't be scared; be skilled! I can't urge you strongly enough to take a course in self-defense. The training will give you so many ways to protect yourself in a variety of situations, ways to slow down a would-be attacker long enough for you to get away, that your self-assurance will show. You will give off such strength and confidence that no one will want to mess with you!

This kind of readiness can be compared to putting a theft-prevention device on the steering wheel of your car. We know that a skillful carjacker *could* saw through the metal and drive off in his newly acquired vehicle, but he is more likely to turn away to an easier target. Self-defense courses are offered through senior centers, at community colleges, at high schools, and elsewhere.

If, after having met the person, you have any doubts at all about him, don't allow yourself to be driven to dinner or to the theater. Take your own car. If you have *strong* doubts, don't go! These are reasonable precautions and should keep you safe.

Margaret's Story

"Margaret," an attractive widow in her early sixties, told me about a fellow she met for afternoon coffee at a local open-air shopping mall. The man knew of Margaret's Scottish origins, so he'd put on a tam-o'-shanter with a feather in it, tartan trousers, a tweed jacket with a red handkerchief in the top pocket, and a red tie to match. At first, she found him amusing, but as they talked, his conversation grew more and more "suggestive."

"I've known women like you," he said. "Cool, sexually aloof. And I've had success with them. I will have success with you."

"I had heard about men who undress you with their eyes," Margaret told me, "and this man made it clear he knew exactly which buttons would remove my blouse! Even though he insisted he would never make the first move—that would come from me, he said—I grew more and more uncomfortable. And I knew that I wouldn't risk going out with him. He telephoned a couple of times, always insisting that he would be a `gentleman' if he took me out—he realized his talk had made me nervous—but I didn't change my mind."

Ed's Story

Not only women, but men, too, have some reservations about entering into possibly dangerous situations. One man—"Ed"—told me his doubts about going to meet a woman who responded to his newspaper advertisement. The two spoke on the telephone at some length before the woman divulged that she lived at Big Bear Lake, a region reachable by road in winter only during the day, when the ice on the roads thawed. As soon as evening fell, the ice would form again, and he would have to wait until the next day before returning down the mountains.

The woman invited him to stay overnight in her spare room—*really* risky on her part, as she knew nothing about him except what he chose to tell her. She would cook him dinner and breakfast, she promised, if he would agree to make the journey.

But what if the woman was after his body? What if he were assaulted by thieves in her house? What if it was a setup to relieve him of his wallet, or even his life? He pondered all these possibilities in advance of setting off on his adventure up the mountains—but not before telling his adult daughter exactly where he was going and when he expected to return!

As it turned out, he had no need to fear for his safety. The problem was that the lady proved a most unlikely match. "She was a nice person but physically most unsuitable for me. I'd told her I'm slightly built, but she gave me no indication of how large she was! She towered over me, especially as she piled her hair so high it was like a tower atop her head. She also wore *powerful* perfume, perfume that permeated the house, competing with the strong smells of frying. And I was stuck until the next day. I felt *so* uncomfortable, sorry I'd made the trip, sorry to be so ungrateful for her efforts to please me. If we'd been able to meet locally for coffee, we'd have known immediately we were wrong for each other and we could have ended it quickly." Another risk then, a minor one, is of wasting everyone's time!

We will deal at some length with sexual behavior and sexual expectations in the new world of dating in Chapter 7, but we have to include sexually transmitted diseases in any discussion of physical danger to people who are dating, no matter what their age.

Since the sexual revolution on the 1960s, both women and men have expressed themselves sexually much more freely than they did in the past. With this new freedom, we have seen increases in sexually transmitted diseases of epidemic proportion. And where it was once mostly men who contracted these diseases—servicemen, travelers, and so on—now women have equal opportunity.

Some of these diseases are incurable, although not deadly. Genital herpes is one such condition. You'll sometimes see this information divulged in personal advertisements so only similarly affected people will respond. AIDS (as well as HIV, the virus that causes AIDS) is incurable and deadly, and it is spreading throughout the community.

You can never assume that a person is not infected, and if you engage in sexual intercourse or any other intimate sexual activity with someone new, you will be *safer* using a latex condom, but not necessarily *safe*. A condom can break, in which case the disease may be transmitted. In the movie *Secrets and Lies*, a young woman intimates to her friend that she and her lover had used two condoms—which would have further added to the safety—but she confessed they used them consecutively, not simultaneously!

Present knowledge is that AIDS is transmitted only when certain bodily fluids—semen or blood, for example—are exchanged. AIDS is not transmitted by casual kissing or, apparently, even by deep kissing. Oral sex, however, is risky, and some STDs can be passed along in this way.

According to Beth Baker and Susan L. Crowley, in the *AARP Bulletin*, Americans over fifty may want to pay more attention to the AIDS problem. Over thirty-four thousand people over fifty, more than 10 percent of infected Americans, have full-blown AIDS. Persons at risk are those who use intravenous drugs or have multiple sex partners or have a partner who practices unsafe sex, has had a blood transfusion, or uses drugs. "Other Americans over fifty are potentially at risk, sometimes without realizing it, when they begin dating following a divorce or the death of a spouse."

A survey by researchers Stall and Catania found that older Americans are one-sixth as likely as younger people to use condoms. They seem not to perceive themselves at risk, and this can have serious repercussions.

But what is a woman to do if the man can't sustain the necessary erection to use a condom? Insist that he have an HIV test! Be warned, though, that the test is actually for antibodies to the virus, and antibodies do not develop for six to twelve weeks after infection. This means a person can test negative—yet can infect a sexual partner. The only way to be sure a negative result is true is for the person to be celibate during this window period of up to twelve weeks before taking the test.

A man, too, may insist that a woman with whom he intends to have a sexual relationship also take an HIV test, so be prepared for that. Only you know what you have been up to sexually, and given these dangerous times, the request is not unreasonable; it isn't a slur against your character. The likelihood that a woman will transmit the disease to a man is much less than that a man will transmit it to a woman, but it is possible.

Jean's Story

Among some people, AIDS awareness is high, as shown by the story told by "Jean."

"I was seeing this nice man. We'd been out several times, and I invited him to my house for a home-cooked meal. I also invited `Peggy,' my twenty-eight-year-old, unmarried daughter, who lives nearby, to join us.

"My daughter saw the man reaching across the table to squeeze my hand—his way of complimenting the chef, I suppose—and jumping entirely to the wrong conclusion, she blurted out, `I hope you guys are using condoms. These days, you can't be too careful.' The man was absolutely mortified. He turned beet-red and muttered, `Oh, jeez!'

"I could hardly contain myself, and as soon as he'd left the house, I burst out laughing, thinking about the poor guy's discomfort and the whole role-reversal thing—having my daughter talk to us like a parent—not that my mother or father would have *dreamed* of talking to me and a boyfriend like that! It also made me realize that younger single people take sex for granted in a way I never did—or could!"

You may never take casual sex "for granted," but if you are contemplating a new sexual relationship, you really *can't* be too careful. While AIDS can be deadly, other sexually transmitted diseases such as herpes, gonorrhea, and chlamydia can be devastating. Have regular medical checkups and frank discussions with your gynecologist about your sexual activity and ways to stay healthy.

"It's all very well," I can hear you say, "insisting that a man use a condom or be tested for HIV, but how am I to do that?"

Perhaps you would rather just be "spontaneous" and let a kiss lead to a caress and then to another caress—and finally to bed. But this is not the time to leave things to chance or to be coy, no matter how shy or embarrassed you feel about raising the issue of protection. Young people have some bold slogans: "No glove, no love!" being one of them. You don't have to be quite as forthright, but it is perfectly acceptable these days to mention the dangers and to suggest that both of you need to be protected.

PROTECTING YOURSELF AGAINST FINANCIAL RISKS

Not all older people are well off, but many widows and divorced women have accumulated substantial assets. Mortgage insurance may mean the house is paid for—free and clear—and other policies may have left a widow with money to invest. Divorce settlements in joint-property states may also result in sizable holdings or income. But even the less well-off can be victims of scams of all kinds and can be preyed upon by the unscrupulous.

§ Keep your financial situation to yourself.

§ Be wary of too many questions about your assets.

§ Keep your assets in a trust.

§ Don't be persuaded to invest without full investigation.

Again, you will be safe if you take precautions. Be alert! Do not tell too much too soon. If a suitor seems overly interested in knowing about your finances, let him know that your assets are held in trust and cannot be touched without consultation with your accountant, your children, your priest, your rabbi, or anyone else you can think of!

If he continues to be curious, be suspicious. Do not be persuaded to put money in any stocks or funds without first investigating them fully. And if marriage talk is in the air, discuss prenuptial agreements. Any honest person will consider this reasonable—and will want his own assets to be protected too.

When I asked "Karen" why she had signed up with a matchmaking service and paid the incredibly high fee of twenty thousand dollars, she said it was because she was afraid of being defrauded. Two of her equally rich women friends had met and married men who later were discovered to be financially insolvent. One was heavily in debt. Karen felt the kind of investigation into clients' finances this matchmaker conducted would safeguard her assets.

You can, of course, do some sleuthing yourself into a prospective partner's finances, if you feel it necessary. You can hire a private detective on your own. Further, you can get a great deal of information about people through public, not private, sources without paying the many thousands of dollars charged by matchmakers, if you know how to track it down. The inset on page 119 provides you with a list of books that can help you investigate a person's history. Indeed, very few match-

---

VERIFYING PERSONAL INFORMATION

If you have ever applied for a job, bought a car or a house, applied for a credit card, renewed your driver's license, or looked into your family tree, public records exist on you! Several books offer both general resources and step-by-step instructions on how to investigate a person's financial, marital, criminal, and business history.

Find Public Records Fast: The Complete State, County, and Courthouse Locator, 1997, Facts on Demand Press, 1997. (Write to 4653 South Lakeshore Drive, Suite 3, Tempe, AZ 85282, or call 800-929-3811.)

Dennis King, *Get the Facts on Anyone*, Macmillan, NY, 1995.

Kevin Sherlock, *How to Be Your Own Detective*, Flores Publications, 1993. (Write to P.O. Box 830131, Miami, FL 33283-0131.)

When in Doubt, Check Him Out, Hallmark, North Miami, FL, 1993.

---

makers claim to protect clients' finances. Their contracts usually contain disclaimers about personal or financial injury sustained in the course of meeting and dating one of their "matches."

PROTECTING YOURSELF AGAINST EMOTIONAL RISKS

Many of us are alert to the possibility of physical hurt, but we are rarely ready for the emotional hurt that can be experienced by people who are dating. We think because we are grown-up, we can cope in ways that young people cannot.

§ Love can be painful at any age.

§ Know what kind of commitment will work for you.

§ Know how willing you are to compromise.

§ Know how much to trust.

§ Feel assured that you can deal with rejection.

"Love makes fools of the very young—and the very old," so goes the old saying. I would argue that love can make fools of us at *any* age and that older, more "experienced" people are not immune. We should know, too, that it isn't only women who get hurt. Intentionally or not, we women can cause serious emotional pain, as several men confided.

John's Story

"John" was a virgin when he married, as was his wife, and he did not believe in sexual intercourse without the blessing of the church. He and his wife felt so strongly about this that when they learned their daughter had gone to bed with her boyfriend, they threw her out of the house!

At sixty-two, John was suddenly left a widower, and given his strong feelings about sexual behavior, he was desperate to remarry, if he could find someone suitable.

"I went to a dance, and we did line-dancing—you know, men and women alternate in the line and each holds the neck or shoulders of the person in front. I can't tell you how wonderful it was to feel a woman's hands on my neck. It had been so long."

He met a woman he liked a lot, but her views about sex were different from his.

"She persuaded me into bed. I actually made love to someone outside of marriage. I'd never done that in my life. I was sure she would marry me—how could she not, having gone to bed with me? But she eventually made it clear she didn't want to marry. Not me or anyone else. I felt terrible—dirty, used. I know it's women who usually say those things, but I really felt that way, feel that way. I loved her too, or thought I did. I would never have slept with her if I hadn't. I found myself crying a lot, crying for my lost innocence, in a way, crying for my wife. I miss her so much. I don't think I'll ever find someone who thinks the way I do about these things."

Harold's Story

Several of my male interviewees conveyed the same sense of having been betrayed by women. Another widower, "Harold," in his mid-seventies, fell seriously in love and wondered why the lady never asked him to her home, always going to *his* house. She kept telling him what a wonderful cook she was, but he was never able to sample any of the dishes she talked about.

"She was about sixty-five and in wonderful shape. A really beautiful woman, plump and feminine. I called her `comely.' I found myself thinking about her all the time. I'd wake up in the morning, or in the middle of the night, and I'd hold conversations with her as though she was there.

"I did something really out of character for me. Instead of taking her to bed in my own house, I took her to New Orleans for a romantic weekend. It was marvelous! We were like a pair of young honeymooners. I thought my dating days were over—and good riddance!—and I could settle down with this lady for the rest of our lives. And then she told me she was married, unhappily, to someone she would never divorce.

"She was using me for diversion, for sex, for fun. In *My Fair Lady*, a song asks why a woman can't be more like a man. Well, some of the women are doing to men what men used to do to women: using them and discarding them. It was all a waste of time for me, time I could have used looking for the right lady. After all, time is not on my side."

Men, it seems, are not so different from women when it comes to emotional hurt, but perhaps we women are especially vulnerable. In *The Cemetery Club*, a film about three widows in their fifties and sixties, an always remarrying older woman says, approximately, "Women our age don't fall in love. It's too painful. Like our thin bones, our hearts are thin too and easily hurt and damaged." Esther, one of the widows, played by Ellen Burstyn, does fall in love and is hurt by a man who "can't make a commitment lasting more than twenty minutes."

The lament that men these days—and women too—"won't make a commitment" is heard among single people in all age groups. Esther, the Burstyn character, finally comes to terms with her lover's reluctance to marry and settles for a kind of "permanent temporariness." It's clear that the man cares for her and wants to be with her, as she wants to be with him, but that he is terrified of being tied down. Like many older women, and some younger ones, Esther finds she must adjust her philosophy to suit the circumstances.

Changed expectations cause considerable anguish. A woman who has been secure in a marriage of many years takes permanence and assurance for granted. She may expect to remarry if the right man comes along and have the same kind of life she enjoyed before she was widowed, but the man of her choice has other ideas.

"I didn't want to be his date, or his *girlfriend*," one woman, "Martha," told me. "I wanted to be his *wife*, and I wasn't prepared to settle for less. So I told him I wouldn't see him again. It nearly broke my heart. After years of grieving for my husband, I felt as though I was bereaved again. I don't remember ever feeling quite so lost and unhappy."

Mature people fall crazily in love, just as younger people do, and suffer just as much from breaking up as if they were teenagers. The emotional suffering can, in fact, be even more profound in the later years than for younger people. A compounding of losses in later life can lead to a sense of hopelessness and despair, a feeling that the last chance at happiness has been taken away.

Compromise is possible: a willingness to let go of old, perhaps outmoded, patterns and accept different ways of living. Martha did eventually rejoin the man she loved. Many months apart did not ease her longing for him, or his for her. "I decided life is just too short. We have to take joy where we find it, and being with him, even on his terms, is a joy—far better than being without him." She still would like to persuade him into marriage one day, but knowing how he feels about "being tied down," she has become more relaxed about taking each day as it comes instead of planning far ahead.

The man in Martha's life has been honest with her; he has made his intentions clear. She knows the score and, eventually, has come to accept it.

There may be circumstances that simply are not acceptable, and knowing the score should encourage you to move out of the relationship. Sometimes children—yours or his—may intrude in ways that make marrying or living together impossible.

Gladys' Story

"Gladys," one of the women whom I interviewed, seriously considered marriage to "Morgan," a man with whom she thought she had a great deal in common—until she met his daughter. This woman, in her early forties, still felt angry and betrayed by her parents' late-life divorce, even though it had occurred many years before. She was rude to Gladys, refused to attend events if Gladys was to be present, and generally behaved like a resentful adolescent, even though her parents' divorce had had nothing to do with Gladys.

Morgan, rather than supporting Gladys during his daughter's screaming attacks on her, sided with his daughter and blamed Gladys, insisting that she was not compassionate enough, that she didn't understand about fathers and daughters and the bond between them. After months of verbal abuse from Morgan's daughter, Gladys decided the problem could not be resolved, and she reluctantly broke off her liaison with Morgan.

In other cases, resentment from adult children may simply stem from fears that they might lose financially. It is not unknown for a parent to change his or her will when a new love comes along and children may be worried that some wily man or woman will strip them of the inheritance they think is "rightly" theirs. If these matters are not cleared up satisfactorily, plans to marry may not be realized.

Knowing How Much to Trust

When I was growing up, I believed my father when he said "A gentleman's word is his bond," and I still believe him. My father was honorable in business and in other areas of his life, as was my husband and as are my brother and my sons.

Now, though, I have learned to be a little more cautious. Some of the men I have met in recent years laughed out loud when I recited my father's phrase. "Words don't mean anything!" one man told me, "especially in business, especially between men and women." He indicated that you could only rely on what people did, not on what they said.

Whether people are telling the truth or not, words do mean something! The people who hear them are affected by them and act upon them. To complicate the matter further, people hear selectively. That is, they hear what they want to hear and turn a deaf ear to the rest.

A man may tell you he loves you but that he doesn't want to make a commitment. Hear him—listen to the last part especially, even if you would rather block it out or believe he doesn't mean it. Yes, he may change his mind at some later date, but you can't depend on that, and you may save yourself considerable anguish if you accept his words at face value.

The problem of how much to trust any other person is not easy to solve. Real trust comes with time, with enough experience of a person to know that his actions match his words, that he really *does* mean what he says. Meanwhile, the trick is not to be swayed by a man's charming statements or by your own longing to believe what you hear.

Dealing With Rejection

Rejection is a serious risk for women and men who are dating. Rejection is painful at any age; for the older person, newly returning to dating, it can be devastating. "If you stick your neck out, you must expect to get your head chopped off!" The fear of getting one's head chopped off is enough to keep some people at home watching television or knitting.

It helps if we avoid taking rejection too personally and remember what one of the matchmakers told me: Only about one person in two hundred will be a compatible partner for any man or woman. Put differently, "You have to kiss an awful lot of frogs before you find a prince!"

Each of us represents one of many possibilities for the person we are just meeting. It is against all the odds that the first person we meet, or the second, or even the tenth or twelfth, will be our soul mate, or that we will be the one in two hundred for him.

You will meet a man, have pleasant, or not so pleasant, conversation for an hour or so, and never see, or want to see, that person again. And he will feel the same about you. This does not mean you are undesirable or that you will never find someone whose tastes and interests are in tune with yours. Sometimes you will meet someone with whom you do feel an affinity—but he doesn't appear interested in you, doesn't suggest another meeting, and seems eager to draw your meeting to a speedy close.

It's easy to take this as personal rejection, to feel hurt and to want to retreat from the game forever. But remember that some of the men you meet may have been searching for a partner for a long time. You may be the seventy-seventh woman a man has met for coffee, and he has learned to cut quickly through the superficialities. Or he may have received eighty responses to a personal advertisement and is merely "weeding out" the unlikely ones. A man may even arrange to meet you at a given time and in a designated place, and then not appear. Being stood up is not pleasant, but it happens now and then.

"Edgar" shamefacedly told me of arriving at a restaurant, seeing the lady sitting on a bench, as arranged, and turning on his heel and leaving before she caught sight of him. "I felt terrible about it. It was a rotten thing to do, I know, but she was so far from my type, physically, I knew it would be a waste of time. She sounded likely on the telephone, but at my time of life, I know I like a well-toned, athletic kind of woman, and she just wasn't interesting to me."

I must confess my own shame at rejecting more than one pleasant man because he was not my "type." After a long and delightful telephone conversation with "Samuel," an artist who had responded to my advertisement in *The Nation*, we arranged to meet in Chinatown for a *dim sum* luncheon. "My son persuaded me to answer your ad," he said. "And when I told him we were meeting, he said `I hope she has a kind heart.'"

I polished my kind heart until it shone, but despite our enjoyable telephone conversation, I found our first meeting disappointing. Physically, Sam was just not my type. For example, he had long, rather sparse hair that he wore in a ponytail, while

I really prefer men with a more clean-cut, tidy appearance.

I so much enjoyed his stories about his travel and his work that I decided not to give up on the relationship right away. Looks don't matter, I kept telling myself—as I tell other women! Character is far more important. When he telephoned me a day or so later, I agreed to go to a movie and a meal with him. I felt I owed this good man another try. Again I greatly enjoyed his company, and the film was good and the meal tasty—but I knew by this time that there would be no future together for us.

I should add that this man, a widower, had been happily married for long time to a woman who adored him and had, therefore, been loveable and attractive to someone and would undoubtedly be found so again by someone else. Much as I would have liked to continue our friendship, I felt it would be unfair of me to lead him on, fairer to let him down gently.

While I encourage people not to give up too quickly on a new relationship, you really need not feel guilty about refusing to see, or continue seeing, someone who clearly doesn't meet your needs. You have a reasonably good idea of what you would like to find in a partner, and you would be serving neither yourself nor the other person by continuing along a path that was leading nowhere.

A man who did make me feel sad was a professor who invited me to lunch at his faculty club, even though he must have known he was opening himself up to rejection. He was a delightful telephone conversationalist, and we appeared to have a lot in common. He said he was in his early sixties, but as soon as I saw him, I knew he was in his mid- to upper-seventies.

He was semiretired, teaching just one course a year. He had warned me that he was completely hairless, so I was not surprised at his bald head and lack of eyebrows, but he had not told me that he could barely walk and had had major surgery on his hips that had not eased the condition. I gently reminded him that my advertisement had mentioned finding a companion to hike with, but he dismissed that need as superficial. "A person like you has a life of the mind. That's much more important than the physical!"

He was so unwilling to let me go, so eager to hold on to me for an hour or two longer, that he begged me to come to his university office so he could show me some of his book and manuscript collections. I wanted to get away but felt it was a kindness to stay a little longer. Finally, as I prepared to leave, he asked me to drive him home as he had no car. He had promised his deceased wife that he would never drive the city streets. Even had I been interested in seeing this man again, it would have meant acting as chauffeur in our city of minimum transport.

Rejection need not be brutal. Busy people can claim their full work schedules as an excuse not to make any dating plans for a while. As I mentioned in an earlier chapter, another device to cut off a would-be suitor kindly is to claim the return of a long-lost love: "Someone I used to care for has come back into my life." This may be a tad transparent to anyone with much experience of dating and may be recognized for what it is. "I really enjoyed meeting you; you're an interesting person; but I don't think we really have much in common" will do in a pinch if you are sure you want to end a relationship before it begins.

You open yourself to rejection whenever you make the first call after an initial meeting. Women are particularly reticent about calling a man for another meeting after having coffee together. "We had this wonderful couple of hours together, so engrossed in each other we didn't see anyone else around us. The most interesting man I've met for a very long time. Then, he didn't call! What should I do? I liked him so much. He said he'd like us to go to the movies together and that he'd telephone to arrange it. And he hasn't."

If you do decide to call a man you like, you should be prepared to have the man not even remember who you are! Carol Burnett, speaking to a room full of students at the Actors Studio in New York, told them not to take it personally if they didn't get the part they had auditioned for. "It just means you aren't the right type." It's as simple as that. You may just not be that particular man's type—but you will be the right type for someone else. Don't take the early phases of getting to know someone too seriously!

The youngish proprietor of a matchmaking agency, herself terribly eager to meet a man, marry, and have children before she hit forty, told me of her concentrated effort to find the right partner. She advertised, followed advertisements, went to singles mixers, attended singles seminars, did everything she could to place herself where that elusive man would be.

"In one year, I met and went out with several hundred men! Can you imagine? *Hundreds* of men! I was meeting three or four on one day! It became my work, my life, my relaxation, my entertainment, and finally, excruciating drudgery. It got so all the faces ran together. I couldn't remember who was who. I liked that one's looks, that one's income, that one's jokes, that one's voice, that one's politics . . . but it all became impossible. I couldn't have made a decision about any one of them if my life depended on it!"

Now, while few of the men you meet will be "interviewing" many hundreds of potential mates in a year, they are probably having coffee with several people each month. A call from you may delight a man, remind him of how much he enjoyed your company, and bring forth an invitation to the movies or to dinner. Or it might not! It's up to you to decide if you are willing to chance it.

Life is a risky business. You take your chances every time you step into the street or climb into a car. Facing the physical, financial, and emotional risks of dating and mating in later life, and knowing how to avoid them, reduce them, or get rid of them completely, will allow you to enjoy your adventures fully and confidently.

Chapter Seven

To Bed or Not to Bed, That Is the Question

Whenen I was growing up, in my lower-middle-class community "nice" girls were not supposed to know anything about sex. In fact, just before my wedding, I asked my mother if there was something I should buy or do to be prepared. "I mean, I don't want to get pregnant straight away," I said.

My mother waved my question away with "*You* don't have to do anything. Let your husband take care of that."

The outcome of that advice was that I got pregnant in the first week of my marriage. My young bridegroom, as ignorant as I in these matters, didn't know that he had to withdraw quickly after ejaculation, so the condom he was wearing slipped off and nature took its course. Perhaps for the best, that pregnancy ended after a few weeks, and we had time to learn a bit about birth control.

When women in the family had babies, the unmarried girls—young women—were not let in on the details of the deliveries, especially if they were difficult or unusual deliveries. Voices dropped to a whisper if an unmarried girl entered the room when these things were being talked about.

To say that society has changed in this regard in the last several decades is an understatement: Society has been transformed.

The once unmentionable is talked about openly and, it some-times seems, endlessly. Television advertisements bring the most private aspects of the female reproductive system into our living rooms. Over dinner or while we sip our evening coffee, we must hear all about the advantages of sanitary napkins with "wings," "vaginal moisture that lasts for days," and perfumed "feminine hygiene" products—unless we choose to flip the switch.

Movies were once governed by the Hays Production Code. This meant that we saw only closed-mouth kisses on the screen and that movie husbands and wives slept in separate beds. If married couples were shown in a double bed, one foot—the man's or the woman's—was to stay firmly on the floor. The camera left the room if love-making was indicated, and the audience was left to imagine what was taking place. It was very discreet—and very romantic.

An old professor of mine told me about his fraternity initia-tion back in the 1950s. One of the endurance tests was the watch-ing of a pornographic movie. He described the dismay of the naive initiates as they watched the events on the screen, and the urgent clambering over bodies in the dark as he, and a couple of other young men, struggled to get out—before they threw up!

Now, the same kinds of movies are routinely rented for a small fee and are watched—one trusts only by adults—in the living rooms of ordinary families of all social classes. Sex acts are depicted in mainstream films in sweaty detail. Condom use is demonstrated in high school, junior high school, and even ele-mentary school classrooms, bananas standing in, or standing up, for penises. This is the post-sexual-revolution era.

The sexual revolution that began in the 1960s and that accompanied the movements for civil rights, women's liberation, and gay liberation, wiped out most of the sexual inhibitions and prohibitions many women grew up with. Younger women, espe-cially, demanded an end to the double standard that allowed men to have sexual experiences outside marriage but didn't allow that same privilege to women. Women need not now "save themselves" for marriage. They had equal rights to orgasms and to sexual pleasure with multiple partners. They also had equal rights to the sexually transmitted diseases that ran rampant.

Epidemics of, for instance, genital herpes, chlamydia, and now AIDS have put a crimp in the sexual revolution. But the Pandora's box of sexually transmitted disease has been opened, and there's no putting the lid back on. Sexuality, sexual expression, and sexual needs are no longer subjects to be only whispered about. And caution in sexual exchanges *must* be discussed. It may be a matter of life or death.

NOT ALL WOMEN WERE EQUALLY AFFECTED BY THE SEXUAL REVOLUTION

The first of the boom babies, who began turning fifty in the mid-nineties, grew up during the years of sexual revolution and may take some sexual freedom of expression for granted. Most long-married women in their upper fifties and sixties grew up with vastly different expectations of how decent girls expressed themselves sexually. Back then, "nice girls" didn't, or, if they did, they kept quiet about it!

These women, single again, are still "nice girls," not comfortable with the idea of sex outside marriage and not sure what men, nowadays, expect of them. A beautiful woman of sixty-five, widowed for five years, told me she is "dating" two people; neither of these friendships is "romantic," she said.

"I would love to have a companion, although living alone has its advantages. I would like to be someone's special someone. But I just can't imagine going to bed with anyone. I just can't picture any of the men I know . . . I mean, our relationships are not sexual at all. With one of them . . . we did kinda dabble, but it was just so uncomfortable we didn't pursue it. I don't even know if any of my men friends . . ." she indicated uncertainty about their sexual powers. "You know, sex wasn't all that important, even in my marriage. Not a big part of our lives. People didn't go on about it all the time, the way they do now."

Another woman I interviewed, though, in her late sixties, who has been twice widowed, has had several love affairs, both between husbands and since her second widowhood. For her, sex is the stuff of life. "I have never been without it."

When I first interviewed her, she was very much in love with a man she had met through a personal advertisement. He was talking of marriage, but she wasn't sure yet, she said, how the affair would resolve itself. She expressed some doubt about how long she could go on attracting new partners as she grew older.

Given her willingness to be "out there," as she put it, I suspect she will continue to find lovers as long as she wants them. It is this willingness that makes a difference. My doctor recently told me a lovely story about her mother. "She's always had a romantic life," she said, "and she's just getting married for the third time, for love, and she's nearly eighty."

These women's varied experiences and views support the research into sexuality that shows that patterns of sexual activity continue from youth to very old age. Those who enjoyed frequent or regular sexual activity earlier in their lives continue to enjoy it—if they have a partner or partners to share it with—while those for whom sexual activity was of little importance or unsatisfying or even distasteful are content to let that part of their lives diminish and cease as they grow older, even if they are married. But even those whose sex lives were dull can be stirred to sexual excitement with a passionate and patient new lover.

WHAT IS APPROPRIATE SEXUAL BEHAVIOR?

The rules about doing something about one's sexual desires are not necessarily clear or rigid. What you decide depends on the situation—and it isn't always easy to interpret the other person's feelings or expectations and behave appropriately. In one case, a man may be delighted if a woman indicates a sexual interest in him. In another instance, he may be completely turned off.

Herbert's Story

"Herbert," an old acquaintance, told me of his pleasure at being invited to a home-cooked meal with a woman he had known for a couple of months. They had been to the movies and the theater together several times, and he thought of her as a good friend.

She had set an elegant table, with beautiful silver and flowers and candles. The food was excellent, the conversation was interesting, and the music on the stereo set a gently relaxed and romantic mood. After the meal, the woman suggested they move to the living room, where she promptly inserted a tape into the video player—a pornographic movie!

Herbert was shocked. He was offended by the film and offended that the woman took such an assertive and "coarse" lead in moving the relationship along. "I simply left. Walked out. Never saw her again and never wanted to."

David's Story

According to most of my male interviewees, such a blatant come-on by a woman is far from usual. A widower, "David," said he had fully expected women to be sexually assertive. "My single men friends told me that all the women are sex-starved and are ready to go to bed at the drop of a hat. This hasn't been my experience at all. Mostly, the women seem quite content to be just friends, companions, to go out for dinner and pleasant walks. They don't seem sex-starved to me. I wish more of them were! I never know how a woman will respond to sexual overtures. It's always a delicate matter."

He was propositioned by one lady fairly soon after they had met. It was a "cute meet"—a meeting between people in unlikely but pleasant circumstances. He was waiting at the appointed time at the foreign languages section in a bookstore for a woman who had responded to his personal advertisement in the local paper. He'd spoken with her on the telephone but didn't know exactly what she looked like.

A woman who seemed "likely" came through the door at precisely the time of the arranged meeting.

"Are you `Patricia'?" he asked her.

"No, my name is `Emma,'" she said.

"Oops! Sorry. I'm supposed to meet a woman here, and I don't know what she looks like. I thought you might be her."

The woman smiled and moved away, through the bookstore. A few moments later, she came back. "I'm not Patricia," she said. "But will I do?"

Although David had really liked the look of this woman, he found the situation embarrassing. The other woman was due any minute. "So Emma gave me her card and said I should call her if I was interested in getting together for coffee sometime."

He did call Emma a few days later, and they soon became friends. "She told me she was willing to go to bed with me—but she set up some very rigid rules on the relationship. It was to be exclusive. I was to spend every weekend with her and three nights out of the five week nights. Also, I was to call her every day."

"Was that acceptable?" I asked.

"No. Not at all. I'm afraid I laughed at her. I said this reminds me of Shaw's *Don Juan in Hell*. Don Juan didn't want to be cut off from half the human race, and nor did I."

Emma had not estimated the situation correctly. While exclusivity in a sexual relationship is an understandable expectation, to insist on such loverlike attention from a man before there have been professions of affection and a wish for exclusivity on his part may nip in the bud any prospects for anything closer than friendship. Feelings of commitment must be mutual, and mutually expressed.

Many men I spoke with had some kind of informal agenda establishing when a friendship should progress to sexual expression. Usually, it was after four or five dates. "Men our age are adults, not children," one interviewee told me. "A relationship has to move on or end. I'm not going to pay for theater tickets and expensive meals indefinitely; I'm not courting without getting what I need."

For some women, going to bed after four or five dates, a few weeks, was much too soon. "When he said he wanted to go to bed with me, I was so nervous," one woman, "Janet," told me. "I'd never slept with anyone but my husband, and I didn't know what to expect. I liked him so much, but after *four weeks*! It's such an intimate thing to do, so soon. I'd known my husband a year before we married, and we hadn't had sex. Poor guy! Years later, we laughed about it. He said he'd absolutely *ached*. After an evening with me, kissing and cuddling, he couldn't stand up straight, he needed release so badly. I didn't understand then. Now I do understand, but it's hard to break life-long habits. Beliefs. I still feel he'll lose respect for me. And if this doesn't work out, how many men will I go to bed with? It would make me feel . . . dirty. It goes so much against my grain."

Now, just as in "the old days," you, like Janet, have every right to maintain your standards. You need not feel pressured into giving in to a man who might try to make you feel guilty about the "pain" you are causing, or who suggests that you are behind the times sexually. Your needs for self-respect are just as important as his needs for the release of sexual tension.

Beatrice's Story

"Beatrice," a widow of fifty-five, who had been married for thirty-four years, joined a widow's bereavement group soon after her husband's death. "The women in the group talk a lot about how they would like romance, but they aren't venturing out to find it. They stay in their own circles."

Beatrice, though, two years into her widowhood, *was* now having a serious love affair with a man she had known for seven months, and was finding life "confusing" now. "It's so exciting to be in love with someone new. Yet I'm still in love with my husband."

Her husband, fifteen years older than she was, had been married before and brought four children to the marriage. They had two children together—and then Beatrice raised her dead sister's children too, so the house was always full of young people. Her husband was ill for seven years before he died, and for the last five years of his life, the couple had had no sexual life together. "I had no way of knowing that wasn't a normal situation."

Her relationship with her lover, "Jeff," is different from her marriage. They concentrate on themselves, on each other. They do not live together yet, although they may do so when they both retire. Both are independent; Beatrice thoroughly enjoys the relationship, but she is not yet ready to be defined by it.

"I've never had anyone take care of me this way. Jeff is very caring. I want to nurture the relationship. Keep it romantic. Jeff is a romantic. Flowers, candy, gifts. I'm afraid marriage would not be romantic. *My* marriage certainly wasn't, and I'm enjoying this. I'm not ready to give it up."

She told me it was difficult at first to become sexual with Jeff. "I didn't know if my body was attractive. I didn't know if I was aging all right. I initiated the sex. He was very much a gentleman. We went off on a romantic weekend. He's been very patient and gentle. He doesn't have the same sexual appetite that I do, but he is innovative—and he has become very much more interested in sex, he tells me, than he was earlier in his life."

When she and Jeff first slept together, it was away from home, away from the furniture, the pictures, the ornaments, and the bed she had shared with her husband. "Now, I can sleep with him at home. We have talked about moving somewhere else, but we aren't ready yet."

Beatrice's experience and those of others raise a number of issues that concern both men and women looking for, and finding, love—and sex—in later life.

VULNERABILITIES OF MATURE MEN AND WOMEN

There's no question that many an older woman feels nervous and embarrassed at the very prospect of baring her body for a new man. A widow, married for thirty years or more, never doubted her husband's acceptance of her gradual "softening"; but won't a new man compare her to all the firm-bodied women he's been bedding lately? Divorced women, too, especially those whose husbands had taken up with women ten to twenty years their junior, express the same kinds of concerns about their bodies. Self-esteem takes a dive under these circumstances, and women need all kinds of reassurance that they are seen as attractive and sexy.

We live in a society where women of all ages are made to doubt their attractiveness. Walking around Hollywood Lake one morning, I overheard a conversation between two women, one about twenty-five, the other twice her age.

"You're looking really great, `Louise,'" the younger woman said. "Working out is doing wonders for you."

"Well thanks, `Marge.' I appreciate your support," the older woman joked, "but when I look in the mirror these days, I go `Yechhh!'"

"Don't be so dumb!" Marge snapped back. "When I look in the mirror, I say `Yechhh' as well. What woman is ever satisfied with the way she looks?"

It turns out that most older men are realistic about the women they date, accepting and delighting in the less-than-perfect figures of their partners. Moreover, several men I interviewed told me they had made love to women who'd had a mastectomy and that this was not a problem for them. One man said it was the woman's embarrassment over her scars and her constant references to them that made him uncomfortable.

A story in the magazine *Health* gives more evidence of the acceptance by men of a woman's less-than-perfect body. A woman who'd had a mastectomy and reconstructive surgery found it difficult at first to enter into sexual encounters with new partners. To overcome her discomfort, she talked about her experiences publicly and wrote about them. Now, she has adjusted. "I've been sleeping around," the woman jokes and adds that for the most part men have been wonderful. "They are not as shallow as we may think."

Men have their own vulnerabilities as they age, and like women, they also need reassurance that they are desirable and can satisfy a partner's needs, giving and getting sexual pleasure. Much of a man's sense of manhood lies in his ability to perform sexually, and we, as women, need to know that the older man may need an especially understanding and patient lover.

SEXUALITY AND LATER LIFE

So far, only a few researchers have studied sexuality in the older set. The little that was written about it in the past was filled with gloom and doom about waning abilities and diminishing desire. Older people who continued to enjoy sexual activity felt like freaks, believing their behavior was unusual and perhaps abnormal. Mature males indecorous enough to express an interest in women's bodies were seen as "dirty old men."

Sexuality in older people has not been well understood, nor has it been considered of much interest to scientists until recently—and it isn't difficult to see why this has been so. It has been only since the late twentieth century that most of us expect to be old. Not long ago, men didn't live many years after they saw their last child married, if they survived that long, and the gap between the life expectancy of men and women was small.

Now, men and women can expect to live far longer than any generations of the past. Many once-lethal diseases have been more or less eliminated by childhood immunizations, and even that killer of middle-aged men, heart disease, is being brought under control and is taking fewer lives. A couple can now expect to have twenty, thirty, even forty years of active life after they've launched their children into society as separate, independent adults.

This is an entirely new scene, and while gerontologists—those people who study old age—have been busily thinking about the needs of an aging population, they have mostly concentrated on the services needed by an increasingly disabled group.

True, the very old, in their eighties, nineties, and older—the fastest growing of the age groups—will certainly need services if they are to continue living as independently as possible. The experts, though, are beginning to realize that for the rest of us mature adults, sexual activity may play an important part in our lives, depending on physical well-being, attitude, past experience, opportunity, and an understanding of changing needs.

THE PHYSICAL SIDE OF AGING

It's obvious that not everyone ages in the same way. Just look at those men and women in their seventies and eighties jogging on the beach over there! Up on the boardwalk, though, others in the same age range are being pushed along in their wheelchairs by their spouses or attendants.

Contrary to many people's beliefs, however, most of us will live our long lives in relatively good health. And the news is good about people remaining sexually active well into old age.

Indeed, some women really begin to enjoy making love only after menopause, when they're no longer afraid of getting pregnant, and they surprise themselves—and their mates—with their passionate abandon! According to *The Janus Report on Sexual Behavior*, the first important study of this subject since the Masters and Johnson landmark work, at no age below ninety were people *not* having sex when they were interested and had a sex partner. People in their seventies, eighties, and nineties who had been experiencing sex continuously reported it is as gratifying as ever. The desire and ability to have sex remain important aspects of their lives with their partners.

What about people without partners, though? Samuel and Cynthia Janus noted that women aged fifty-one to sixty-four reported that after they became widowed or divorced, they did not know how to find a sex partner when they wanted one. It would seem, then, that women especially either don't know how to meet appropriate partners or haven't yet found the courage to do so.

Even with partners, though, both men and women experience hormonal changes as they age, changes that may affect them not only physically but also psychologically and, in turn, affect their level of sexual desire.

Women, Menopause, and Postmenopause

Since the baby boomers began turning fifty in the mid-1990s, interest in menopause has become vocal and public. The largest group of women in this country ever to experience menopause at the same time has made menopause the subject of keen discussion. While in the past, menopause, or "the change," was feared as a condition that sent some women crazy—if only for a while—women now are encouraged to understand exactly what is happening to their bodies, what they can expect, and what they can do to ease any unpleasant symptoms.

Menopause brings a sharp drop in the hormone estrogen. This can lead to some dryness and shrinkage of the tissues in the vaginal areas and to discomfort, even pain, during sexual intercourse. Many gynecologists routinely prescribe hormonal replacement therapy (HRT) for menopausal and post-menopausal women, therapy that also helps to strengthen bones, which become thinner as the body's production of estrogen declines.

Some women are uneasy about beginning a therapy that, once started, should be continued for the rest of their lives. Doctors usually advise women that any gain in bone density will soon be lost if the treatment is stopped. Bone loss will continue apace from then on. And while estrogens are known to protect against heart attacks, they pose a slightly increased risk of breast cancer. In the years since HRT was first prescribed for women, the balance of hormones in the pills has been changed: less estrogen, more progesterone. This change lessens the risk of cancer but also reduces the protection against heart attacks. HRT may also have some side effects such as tenderness of the breasts, nausea, and a feeling of "being constantly pregnant," according to some women.

One option to HRT in pill form is estrogen cream dispensed directly into the vagina. Small dosages of estrogen are absorbed into the uterus and other vaginal tissue, helping to moisten the area and thicken the lining of the vagina without the side effects of medicine taken by mouth. Each woman should discuss the positive and negative aspects of all available treatments with her doctor before making a decision. For some women, a non-medical option, such as a dab of KY Jelly or something similar, may just help to get the natural juices flowing, as does regular sexual stimulation.

Men, Aging, and Sexuality

Men do appear to be the more delicate sex in some ways. Unlike women, who experience little sexual impairment with age, a majority of men suffer prostate enlargement: a nuisance that makes for slow, frequent, and sometimes painful passing of urine. The prostate is a small gland that encircles the urethra, through which both urine and semen pass. It produces the seminal fluid in which the sperm swim and in which they are pushed out during ejaculation.

The risk of prostate cancer also becomes greater with age, although those cancers are often very slow growing and cause no problems. Removal of the prostate gland or reduction of the enlargement are fairly common procedures but often leave patients fearing the end of their sexual activity, a fear that is not necessarily based in fact. Prostate surgery, however, like all surgery, has risks, and you may encounter men who have suffered some loss of potency because of it.

Medicines for high blood pressure, sedatives, hypnotics, and tranquillizing drugs may lead to a loss of libido or to impotence. Men—and women too—should ask their doctors about medicines without these side effects. Often, though, the cause is psychological rather than physical. Most specialists believe that the fear of impotence may lead to impotence, and the effect of the mind on the body is of great importance. If, though, the problem is physiological, a number of medical techniques are available, including penile injections, implants, pumps, and so on. Their use depends on a couple's willingness to attempt these possible solutions.

BEING—AND HAVING—AN UNDERSTANDING AND SENSITIVE SEX PARTNER

The woman widowed or divorced after a long marriage she entered, perhaps, when she was young and naive may feel particularly vulnerable to what she sees as "predatory" males—wolves who'll take advantage of her—when she begins dating again for the first time since her teens or early twenties. She may worry that her body is unattractive and not sexy, and that she will be humiliated in some way if she opens herself to a sexual encounter. She may not understand that older men are just as vulnerable to hurt and may be equally afraid of sexual failure and rejection.

Despite their dash and bravado—after all, men are supposed to do the wooing and pursuing—older men may need a lot of encouragement, both verbal and physical, if they are to sexually satisfy themselves and their partners.

So concerned are they with getting an erection and maintaining it that many men may not understand the delicacy needed in their approach to a new love partner. This business of getting an erection is troublesome to men of all ages, almost all of whom have experienced some inability at some point in their lives.

In the delightful film *The Cemetery Club*, Sam Katz, the widower played by Danny Aiello, after ardently courting the widow Esther for several weeks, asks her if she would like him to stay the night. Her confusion—the push of uncertainty and embarrassment and the pull of desire—is real and endearing, familiar to any woman who has been in her situation. Together, the two climb the stairs to the bedroom, and both stare at the bed in which Esther had slept with her beloved husband for forty years. Sam quickly closes the door—and drives Esther away to a hotel. Sam's understanding, and his gentle lovemaking later, indicate a sensitivity to the situation, a delicacy, that one hopes all lovers might display!

Ideally, lovers of any age will try to accommodate to the sexual needs and preferences of their partners, but good loving takes time, as several of my male interviewees told me. Long-married couples sometimes forget how long it was before they achieved mutual satisfaction. One woman confessed that it wasn't until two years after her wedding that she experienced her first orgasm. Another woman told me how she had resisted oral sex for more than ten years "even though my husband longed to kiss me all over and said I was beautiful down there." She said, "I thought sex organs were ugly and dirty and that there was something wrong with him for wanting that."

Other women long to be made love to in that intimate way: "I'd read about it in stories, of course," one widow said, "and wished I could have that experience—but `Frank' would *never* do that. He didn't think decent women would want that—or that they would do it to their husbands. He thought only prostitutes and `loose' women would even *know* about such things."

Given the varied backgrounds, life histories, and expectations of couples coming together in their later years, it isn't surprising that they so often misunderstand and misread each other. Men and women, no matter what their age, often don't understand each other's needs and tend to see sexual activity from different perspectives.

Many men think sexual intercourse is all that sexual activity is about; some women are not as interested in sexual intercourse as they are in being touched and stroked and caressed and, especially, in being told that they are precious and important and loved. These women are not "frigid," and they do enjoy making love—which they may see as separate from "sex." It is important that their partners understand this.

Both men and women say they do the things to their lovers that they would like done to themselves, but these broad hints are not always taken.

One interviewee said, "I wish he would kiss my *back*—from the top of my spine all the way down to my toes. Little kisses. I do that to him and he loves it! But he seems to think that lapping at my clitoris is going to bring me to all kinds of ecstacy. He heads down there before I'm even warmed up. It just makes me sore after a time, especially direct, hard tonguing at the head instead of gentle licking at the sides. And when I ask him to stop, he gets upset and feels rejected and says I make him feel inadequate because he can't satisfy me."

Such lack of understanding can be frustrating and shows a need to talk about what pleases and what doesn't, but few people are comfortable making specific requests of a sexual kind. And expressing, or even thinking, negative thoughts like "You're in your sixties. How can you have learned so little in all those years?" is likely to bring forth that standard male response: "I've never had any complaints before!" The frustrated woman is left feeling guilty for not having orgasm after wild orgasm, the only way, it sometimes seems, for a woman to make a man feel good about his sexual prowess.

A widow of over seventy told me that the man she is very much in love with is unable, because of radical surgery for prostate cancer, to have sexual intercourse but that this in no way diminishes his ability to satisfy her completely. "When we are together, he's making love to me all day," she says. "He kisses my hands, he puts an arm around me, he touches my face in a most intimate way. He strokes my hair. By the time we go to bed, I'm already warmed up, all the juices flowing! He soon learned how to use his hands and his mouth to bring me to orgasm, and this gives him as much pleasure as it gives me."

The older man, even if he has no sexual impairment, is rarely as likely to bruise a woman with hard thrusting of his penis as is a younger man, but he might cause her some discomfort, even pain, in his effort to gain entry with a softer, even flaccid, penis. This is an aspect of lovemaking that women, especially, need to be sensitive to and to understand.

POSITION IS EVERYTHING

Being potent for a man is generally understood as being able to achieve erection, intercourse, orgasm, and ejaculation, in that order. Yet, men tell me, they can be greatly satisfied even when one or two of these elements are missing, or when they occur in different order. For instance, older men are much slower in attaining an erection than when they were younger. This disadvantage is offset by their ability to hold the erection for longer once it is achieved. In some cases, although they "feel" an erection in their heads, the erection isn't evident where it counts! An understanding and patient partner can help a man to "grow," and that may not happen until actual intercourse. This can be a tricky problem, especially at the beginning of a sexual relationship when neither partner knows what to expect. The man knows what he's feeling, knows his history, worries about poor performance and rejection, and so guarantees failure. The woman lies there feeling unattractive and totally lacking in sex appeal.

Can a couple have sexual intercourse if the man does not have an erection or is only slightly erect? In many cases, yes, but face to face positions may not work as well as entry from the rear.

I can hear women all over the country making noises of dismay and even horror at this prospect! "It's like animals!" is a common response when rear entry, or "doggy position," is mentioned. Some think it means anal intercourse, which it certainly does not. Yet, sex experts such as Alex Comfort, author of *The Joy of Sex*, have long recommended rear entry, especially for postmenopausal women whose vaginas tend to shrink somewhat, and for overweight and slightly disabled people, among others. While rear entry is not one of the most common positions for sexual intercourse—some estimates are that around 16 percent of couples use it—it can be gentle on a woman, once the technique is understood, and entry can be made with very little erection or no erection at all. According to Comfort, it can cure partial impotence or nervousness on the man's part by restoring morale. *Before* the position is understood, the idea can cause embarrassment. An attempt can be a pain in the back for a woman, and she can find her face buried uncomfortably in the mattress or the pillow!

Entry can be made either with the man kneeling behind the woman or with both lying on their sides—the "lazy position"—the man curled around his lover's back. Couples will experiment until they find what is best for them. Once inside the vagina, a penis can grow quite large and firm, and the man can proceed in his own time to orgasm, with or without ejaculation. The ejaculate is much sparser in the later years, and the orgasm is sometimes "dry," especially if lovemaking is frequent.

Rear entry does allow the man to manually stimulate the woman, but whether or not she achieves orgasm in that position, she will enjoy the lovemaking and enjoy her lover's pleasure. One woman confided that after intercourse, during which her lover, in his seventies, had a "sensational" orgasm, she experienced a prolonged "sweetness" all over her lower body. "It was a kind of *bliss*, a heavenly, floating sensation, and it lasted for hours, for as long as he remained inside me, which was most of the night. It was far better than orgasm, which is over in seconds, yet it was a kind of orgasm. Gentle and diffused. It was wonderful!"

I learned from several other women that they aren't as desperately anxious about orgasms as their men seem to think they should be. They don't deny that orgasms are important; orgasm can be a wonderful release. But they know it just may take time for their lovers to understand their bodies. Once a woman is brought to orgasm, it becomes ever easier to repeat the performance. In the meantime, women tell me, they are often able to produce their own orgasms through masturbation. What a lover can give them, besides orgasm, or instead of it, is intimacy, closeness, warmth, tenderness, and a sense of security.

No sensible person would suggest limiting positions for intercourse to rear entry. Use any position that is comfortable and pleasurable. Lying face to face with either partner on top, or curling around each other, side by side, tummy to tummy, can be delightful and can greatly enhance feelings of caring and intimacy. Try anything and everything to see what works best.

One fact of life, it seems, is that what works like a charm one time may not work at all next time! "That evening, she was absolutely carried away by the greatest passion you can imagine as I gently stoked her breasts. The next time, I couldn't arouse her at all that way. Or *any* way I tried. Women!"

Lovemaking is an ever-changing experience, a continuing experiment. Trying different kinds of touches—one-time feather-light touches, or tiny pinches and nibbles, or a leisurely head-to-toe massage with baby oil—keeps the excitement alive and new; this works for long-time partners as well as for new lovers. Take a bubble bath together. Make love by candlelight. Snuggle down on cushions in front of a log fire.

And if you are fortunate enough to live in a warm climate, enjoy a hot tub together under the stars. Above all, *talk* to your partner about what pleases and what doesn't. Be willing to try new experiences, but know that you don't have to do anything you don't want to do. And be kind. Giving is also receiving.

Part of the joy of talking with women and men in their fifties, sixties, seventies, and later is the realization that sexual pleasure can be a gift for life. Human beings are both sensual and sexual creatures whose lives are enhanced and enriched by demonstrations of caring and by touching and holding each other, and whose libidos need not disappear with age. Lovemaking among the older set may for some be more deeply gratifying than in youth. At this time of life, couples have time to take their lovemaking slowly. Women and men who were driven sexually in their younger days find they can prolong their delight in each other in ways not previously possible.

Reality Check

Throughout this book, I have been urging you to be realistic. We all have our dreams and fantasies, but if we cling to unreasonable expectations, we are bound for disappointment. My hope is that you are finding the self-confidence to face the new world of dating, that you are experimenting with some of the suggestions I've given you, and that you are beginning to meet compatible people whose company you enjoy.

At this point, you may be starting to consider other questions. For example, are you being realistic in your search for a mate? Is time "running out" for you? Is living together a bad idea?"

THAT OLD BLACK MAGIC:
MORE ABOUT LOVE AT FIRST SIGHT

Attraction to another person is exciting; it gets the juices flowing—but it may have little to do with love. Sexual compatibility can be a wonderful comfort, a reminder and an enrichment of your identity as a woman—but it isn't love. You may think yourself "in love," but you know that the love that lasts is based on much more than physical attraction and sexual satisfaction.

This in no way denies that what we used to call "an affair" can be delightful and fulfilling for some people. In her book, *The Late Show*, Helen Gurley Brown urges older women to keep sexually active, even if it means having sex with some other woman's "mildly unhappy" husband! Sex is separate from love, she writes, and sex with a man, even if you aren't aflame with desire, keeps you "womanly." When Brown was asked how she would feel about having *her* husband serve another woman in this way, she answered that she would kill him!

One of the risks to having an affair, even if your partner is not married to someone else, lies in fantasizing it as "true love." If both partners are realistic about it, they can enjoy themselves for as long as it lasts and not suffer too much emotional damage when it is comes to an end; they might even continue as friends. Too often, though, one partner becomes more emotionally involved than the other, constantly waiting for declarations of commitment that never come, and finally getting badly hurt. And if the man *is* married, you have another set of problems.

"Look," I can hear you protest, "I don't want to have an affair, or a succession of affairs, even if I know that's what they are, and I keep cool about them. I'm looking for a partnership that lasts."

First, then, forget the idea that you will know at first glance that you have met your mate! Not long ago, I was given the pleasant task of writing staff "profiles" for a company's in-house newsletter. In large, bureaucratic organizations, staff members often have no idea of the part their co-workers play in the company, and they certainly don't know much about their personal lives, their hobbies and interests. In my interviews I learned each person's marital status, and of those who were married, I asked for a brief history of their courtship. Whirlwind, swept-off-the-feet romances? There were none.

One woman who had only recently married had known her husband for twenty-two years! They were college sweethearts for four years and then went their separate ways for twelve years before meeting up again. It was another five years before they realized they were "meant for each other."

Another woman, who loved dancing, first met her fiancé in a dance class, then at a dance club where they sometimes danced together. But it took several years before they found they made beautiful music together.

Yet another staff person, planning to marry "before too long," had known his fiancée for four years before deciding she was "the one." Instant love is a bit like "overnight stardom" in show business.

These people all knew that it takes time—although not necessarily several years—for two people to understand each other well enough to make their way together through the thick and thin of everyday life.

BE REALISTIC IN YOUR SEARCH

Being realistic about a potential partner means using the wisdom gained with the years to resist setting impossible standards. Certainly, you may have a "wish list," but you are mature enough to know that no one person can be expected to meet all your needs. You know that you are not perfect, either, and will not live up to another's every expectation. Allow yourself and others to be human. That does not mean accepting someone as a partner if he does not enrich and enhance your life in important ways. It does mean getting rid of fantasies of romance that no human being can provide so that you are bound to be disappointed.

REEVALUATING YOUR NEEDS

Searching for someone new in your life after years, happy or otherwise, with a former husband or lover may mean taking a long, clear look at your present circumstances and, perhaps, broadening the range of men you have previously considered acceptable. Don't deny yourself the opportunity to meet fine men from walks of life other than your own. If your first husband was lawyer, your next husband might nonetheless be a chef or a carpenter. If you thought you were only attracted to men who worked with their hands, you might, nonetheless, find yourself falling for a journalist or a teacher.

If the most important item on your wish list is "academic background and the ability to discuss the philosophies of Hegel and Wittgenstein," clearly you are limiting your options substantially! Perhaps you need to rethink the likelihood of meeting such a person, in your age range, who is also single, who can dance a fancy fandango—another item on your wish list—and who will be bowled over by what *you* have to offer.

The chances are good that you will have to feed your intellectual appetite through a university course, exercise your terpsichorean tastes through a dance class—and modify your expectations of a potential partner if you really want to find one.

A recent article by Janet Kinosian in the *Los Angeles Times* examined successful couples whose tastes in leisure activities ran so counter to each other's that a computer matchmaking program would have "spit the two in opposite directions." In one case, the husband loved opera and studied foreign languages while the wife adored watching the soaps and reading "bodice rippers." Other couples differed even more in their ideas of how to spend their spare time and in the kinds of vacations they enjoyed.

All the couples, happily married for many years, had adjusted their expectations of each other, often taking vacations alone and allowing each other plenty of "personal space." They realized that it was far better, say, for a husband to trek through the wilderness with only the knapsack on his back—if that's what refreshed him and gave him the energy to go back to his twelve-hour work days—than to expect him to accompany his wife to Las Vegas and spend long days and nights at the gaming tables—if that's what pleased *her*. They learned that neither should sacrifice their own enjoyment for the enjoyment of the other and that it is not necessary for couples to march in lockstep through every activity for them to be happy together. Each can agree to be different without loving the other less.

Moreover, good, kind, generous, loving, faithful, understanding men may be found in all occupations. Their interests and hobbies outside work cover the whole gamut, from baseball to Bach. Being realistic does not mean "lowering your standards" if your husband was a professional. On the other hand, women who were married to working men need not feel that men who are in business or the professions are "above them." Women who confine themselves to a narrow segment of the population may be making a real mistake.

"Jim," one of the most interesting men I know, has been an electrician for much of his working life, a union organizer in his youth, a worker for civil rights in the sixties, a lover of classical music and jazz, and a teacher of Tai Chi in his spare time! A woman would not be lowering any standards by becoming the partner of a man like Jim.

MOVE AT YOUR OWN PACE

Let us consider that you know Jim. You met him on a hike, or through a personal advertisement, or at a meeting of the Democratic Club. A nice man, no question about it, whose heart is in the right place. He is concerned about the state of the world, follows political events and plays an active part in registering voters. You like him and admire him. Yet . . .

What do you do if a really fine man like Jim is clearly interested in you and is soon talking about a possible future with you, yet while you are warmed and comforted by his attention, you don't feel for him the kind of affection he feels for you?

An old song goes "A good man nowadays is hard to find," and those words are just as true now as when they were written. You don't want to lose a good man, yet you are not ready, and may never be ready, to be more than a friend to him.

Give yourself—and him—a chance! Let him know that you care about him and that you appreciate his feelings for you but that you are not ready to make a serious decision about sharing your life with him. Don't allow yourself to be rushed or pushed into any commitment you may regret.

Jim may not want to wait, his affection towards you may cool—and your decision will have been made. You'll both move on. On the other hand, he may feel so strongly about you that he is willing to take the chance that, sooner or later, you will care for him as he cares for you.

Months later, Jim's courtship of you bears fruit. You realize he has become central to your life and that most plans you make, and almost every outing you consider, include him and would be empty without him. You are becoming a couple.

The other possibility, though, is that you will grow apart. If you begin to find that, while you still think of Jim as a good person, you'd rather attend a play on your own, you are relieved when he leaves your house so you can relax with a good book, and you are planning a trip without him because you think two weeks of close proximity to him would be overpowering, time may have done its work.

Still, be sure it is really over before you release Jim to some other woman who might appreciate him more than you do. Even long-term, solid partnerships ebb and flow emotionally. Most happily married men and women, if pressed, will admit to times when they would like to be alone, when the strain of domestic life becomes overwhelming and they envy their single friends. Perhaps this restlessness you feel is just part of a normal emotional cycle and will pass.

Remember that adapting to life with another person is easier when you are young and just starting out together. Your tastes and attitudes develop as you spend days and years in each other's company; you get to know each other's funny little ways over time. In a good marriage of many years or decades you agree to disagree; you learn flexibility; you overlook the other's funny little quirks—perhaps you hardly notice them any longer.

At sixty, or seventy, you each have a lifetime of separate experiences. You have become the people you are without any input from, or shared experiences with, the person you are now considering as a partner for the rest of your life. You may find some of each other's habits irritating, and you worry that they may become unbearable.

Still, don't give up too quickly. Take a little break—go by yourself on that trip for a couple of weeks, or on a long weekend retreat. If you soon yearn to see him, you may be more ready to make a commitment than you had thought. If the time you spend on your own brings nothing but relief, make your farewells and start keeping an eye open for someone more compatible!

YOU DO HAVE ENOUGH TIME

We need to face the fact that finding the right partner can take time, perhaps a long time. "But I'm sixty-two, now," I can hear you say. "Next year I'll be sixty-three. Time is not on my side."

Much the same sentiment is sometimes expressed by men and women in their thirties and forties. People of all ages meet and fall in love and make decisions about commitment, and while "time is of the essence" for women nearing the end of their childbearing years, this is not a problem for the over-fifty crowd.

While on jury duty not long ago, I made friends with a fellow juror, a middle-aged woman with teenage children who had recently remarried after many years as a divorcée. Her mother, in her early seventies, she told me with a smile, was *also* newly married, to a man several years younger than she, her first husband having died three years before.

Jerry's Story

My good friend "Jerry" had been actively searching for the right woman since about a year after his wife died four years ago. Retired, he had plenty of time to explore a number of avenues. His personal advertisement appeared week after week, month after month, in the local newspaper. He advertised in magazines with editorial views in tune with his own. He went to discussion groups, and organized his own salons. He took courses, met and dated dozens of women, and generally enjoyed himself.

At times, though, he confided that he was getting really weary of the dating game. The more "ladies" he dated, the more difficult it was to make a decision. Many of the women he met were delightful: "I like this one's sense of humor, that one's smile, that one's lovely voice, this one's intelligence . . ." he would say. But he couldn't seem to find everything he wanted in just one of them.

Then, "Joyce" responded to his newspaper advertisement—and Jerry is on Cloud Nine! He says he feels about this elegant and gracious lady as he has never felt for anyone before. He has met enough women by this time to know that some qualities are more important to him than others. Luckily for him, Joyce cares for him as much as he cares for her. Jerry is seventy-eight years old. I have never heard him refer to his age as any kind of handicap to finding a suitable partner.

Gillian's Story

"Gillian," one of my oldest friends—I've known her some thirty years—had a close liaison with "Bob" for over fifteen years. They had met soon after her second divorce and, although she cared for Bob, because of her past bad experience with marriage, she was not eager to marry him or even to live with him. They kept separate homes in the same town but spent all their leisure time together, including numerous long trips abroad.

Recently, Gillian met "Philip"—at a party she went to with Bob—and the two found they had a lot to talk about together. At the moment, Gillian is dating both Bob and Philip, the men both fully aware of the situation. Bob, seeing the way Philip is pursuing Gillian, is pressing hard for marriage; Philip is attentive and generous and is also pressing for marriage. Gillian is having a wonderful time being ardently courted by two highly eligible men. Is she young and glamorous? She is in her mid-sixties and nice-looking but not particularly a beauty.

So, do not feel that time is running out; do not feel that it is now or never, this one rather than no one at all. Such a level of desperation may, indeed, drive you to settle for someone so wrong for you that "no one at all" would have been the wiser choice.

Take the time to meet and date a large number of potential mates, even though you may at times feel real understanding for the character in the "Crabby Road" cartoon who described dating as like a melting icicle—just one drip after another!

Be prepared, too, for dry spells—perhaps of several months—when you meet no eligible men at all. If you are involved in activities for the pleasure they give you rather than only as opportunities to find a partner, you will enjoy yourself anyway and come away enriched. Part of this enrichment may result from finding people with interests similar to yours and so making new friends. I have added several wonderful women to my circle of friends in the last year or so, meeting them at conversation groups, singles events, and so on, that I was researching as possible resources for people looking for partners.

LIVING TOGETHER: GOOD IDEA OR BAD?

The moral issues of living with a member of the opposite sex without marriage are for you to decide. This arrangement has been commonplace for many years, giving rise to all kinds of earnest discussion about what to call the "roommate." "Significant other"? "Posslque" ("person of the opposite sex sharing living quarters")? "Lover"? Young people often live together for a year or two before marriage, although, contrary to "commonsense" belief, research indicates that couples living together beforehand have slightly higher rates of divorce than couples who did not live together before marriage.

One internationally known matchmaker strongly advises against living together if you really want marriage. There may, of course, be solid reasons *not* to marry—perhaps one of the parties will lose a pension or some other form of income. Otherwise, she asks, why would your partner marry you if he essentially has you as a wife without the commitment involved in declaring your association formally and legally?

More importantly, why settle for living together if what you really want is marriage—since living together does not particularly prepare you for or lead you to marriage? You may have given up your own home and your chance of meeting a serious marriage partner on the hope that the relationship will be permanent. Perhaps it will last as long as you do. But if it fails, you will have lost a great deal emotionally and, perhaps, financially as well.

According to Linda Stern, writing in *Modern Maturity*, "what's mine isn't necessarily yours," when it comes to couples who live together. She cites Mark and Alice as a couple with unequal incomes. Mark was well-to-do and retired while Alice was still working and earning a modest salary. Their relationship fell apart because Mark expected Alice to cater to his expensive tastes on her limited budget. Financial planners urge couples to avoid such unhappy endings by discussing and settling their financial arrangements before they move in together. Unmarried couples are also encouraged to keep their finances separate.

Further, in the event that your live-in partner dies before you, will you be homeless if the house was his and has been willed to his heirs?

If you are wise, you will seek legal advice before setting up home with anyone but *especially* before moving in with someone to whom you are not married.

MARRIAGE WITHOUT LOVE?

In our society, we believe so firmly in the notion of romantic love that we forget, if we ever knew, that marriages were, and still are in some cultures, arranged as a practical matter rather than as the result of passion. These transactions, based on family connections, financial interests, and sometimes simple convenience, appear to have been no less successful than matches based on romantic attraction. In time, the people involved often came to care deeply for one another, even though they were not expected to be "in love" when they said their marriage vows.

This scenario was shown beautifully in the musical *Fiddler on the Roof*, when Tevye begins to think about his relationship with his wife, Golda. Their lovely duet begins when Tevye asks his wife if she loves him. She looks at him as though he's crazy and proceeds to list everything she has done for him over the years: she's cooked for him, cleaned for him, borne his children. . . . He continues to ask her if she loves him. And, finally, although Golda never actually says those words, Tevye concludes that she really does love him.

Given that about 50 percent of marriages now end in divorce, even though they were entered into with great love and high expectations, perhaps some thought might be given to marriage founded on practical considerations.

Before you shake your head right off your shoulders, consider the people for whom a sensibly realistic union might work, even if you have not, before now, thought of such a marriage for yourself.

Grace and Gregory's Story

Grace owned the house in which she and her husband reared their children. When her husband died five years ago, insurance paid off the mortgage but the household expenses were still a struggle to meet on her pension, and she found the property difficult to maintain by herself. Her husband used to look after the garden and the cars while she did the housework and the interior decorating. Now, she sometimes felt overwhelmed with the responsibility of caring for everything. She used a handyman and a gardener sometimes but worried about the cost of even these occasional services.

Grace had considered the options of selling the house and renting a small apartment, or of moving to a less expensive, more manageable house. The thought of either move depressed her. She had lived in her house for thirty years and was comfortable there, knew and liked her neighbors, and did not want to face what she saw as a horrible upheaval of her life.

Gregory, retired on a small company pension and social security payments, was divorced nearly twenty years ago. He had entered into several "relationships" after the divorce, none of which had satisfied him for long. He did not particularly enjoy life on his own, although he had become quite good at cooking, shopping, and cleaning. He lived in a small apartment and worried as the rent increased steadily over the years while his income got smaller.

He had not been "seeing" anyone for several years when he met Grace. They were both lonely; Grace felt she was dwindling into widowhood, missing her life companion and her two grown children, both of whom lived and worked on the other side of the country. She volunteered some time to a local organization working with handicapped children, and it was through that agency that she met Gregory who was also trying to expand his horizons.

They liked each other, but they did not fall crazily in love. They got along well and could be open with each other about their likes and dislikes. They both enjoyed musicals, although neither of them had much money to spare for costly theater tickets. They usually attended inexpensive events and planned visits to local museums and galleries on days when admission was free. They generally paid their own way when they went to movies or ate out, and Grace sometimes cooked dinner for them, Gregory bringing wine or a package of gourmet coffee for a treat.

Neither Grace nor Gregory pretended to be in love, although they soon became the best of friends, and together, they eased much of their loneliness. They took some thrifty trips together and found they remained calm and amicable even during and after long days of driving together in a small, not particularly comfortable car. They shared motel rooms, usually with twin beds, but they did sleep in the same bed at times and enjoyed making love sometimes.

Grace and Gregory dated for a while, perhaps a year or more. As each became more knowledgeable about the other's finances and living arrangements, they began a series of "What if" discussions. "What if you sold your house and . . .?" "What if I left my apartment and . . .?" "What if I moved into your house and I contributed my rent to our shared household instead . . .?" "What if I move in and take over the outside chores . . .?"

After some weeks and months of debating these kinds of questions, they decided they both required a more permanent arrangement than simply moving into the same residence and sharing expenses, although they saw that as a sensible possibility, perhaps a first step. Both had lived in their present homes for a long time and needed to hold onto a sense of security.

As Gregory began staying over at Grace's house for long weekends and then for a week or two at a time, the couple worked out a plan for living together. Both rather private people, they each needed a place to retreat to for solitude. Gregory took the second bedroom as his own bed-sitter and office, though they thought they would sleep in the master bedroom once they were married.

By the time they were married, their living plan was in

place. They share the chores and contribute equally to the food, heating, and other household bills, reducing costs for both of them. They have more money to pay for outside services if they need them. They have companionship when they need it, privacy if they want it, and someone to "be there" if either falls sick or needs some kind of physical or emotional support. The two respect each other, like each other, care about each other, but are still not "in love."

It may be that one need not "fall in love" or "be in love" to care for someone very much and, perhaps, eventually to find one loves the other person. Love is enough of a mystery to allow for all kinds of possibilities, as those arranged marriages of the past demonstrate.

The house remains Grace's property. In her will she stipulates that, if she dies first, Gregory may remain in the house as long as he wishes; after he leaves, or dies, her children will be able to sell the house and share the proceeds.

This kind of marriage may not suit the more romantically inclined, but it is built on firm ground and without illusions.

"What would happen," you may ask, "if either one *does* meet someone else and fall madly in love?" Grace and Gregory have talked about this possibility as they talk openly about any concern. They have concluded that the chances of this are slight. They are not looking outside their marriage for companionship with someone of the opposite sex. Like any couple firmly committed to each other, they have closed off that option. Each lived alone long enough to know that the comfort and security they enjoy together is precious and must not be jeopardized.

The arrangement that Grace and Gregory have designed to meet their needs is just one among many possible ways for couples to share their lives these days. As we live longer, we may become even more flexible in the living styles we consider acceptable and desirable. One soon-to-be married couple I interviewed recently will live much as Grace and Gregory are living, but the wife-to-be has clearly stipulated that the relationship is not to be sexual, her husband-to-be agreeing to this restriction. To judge by their affectionate hand-holding, the two are dear friends. I look forward to talking to them in a year or so to see if anything has changed!

"Being realistic" doesn't mean pushing your dreams aside and settling for something you do not want. Rather, it means understanding and accepting the world as it is.

Being realistic means keeping an open mind and taking time to consider carefully all the possibilities life holds for happiness.

Maturity gives us an edge. We have experienced enough living to appreciate the wisdom of these words excerpted from one of my favorite poems, "After a While" by Veronica Shoffstall, © 1971)

> After a while you learn . . .
> that love doesn't mean leaning
> and company doesn't always mean security.
>
> And you begin to learn that kisses aren't contracts
> and presents aren't promises
> and you begin to accept your defeats
> with your head up and your eyes ahead
> with the grace of a woman
> not the grief of a child.
>
> . . . .
>
> After a while you learn
> that even sunshine burns
> if you get too much
> so you plant your own garden
> and decorate your soul
> instead of waiting for someone to bring you flowers.
>
> And you learn
> that you really can endure
> that you really are strong
> that you really do have worth
> and you learn
> and you learn
> with every goodbye
> you learn . . .
>
> That's "being realistic."

Chapter Nine

Options to Marriage & "Romantic" Love

T he author of one how-to book on finding a husband writes that if you follow her advice, she guarantees that you will be successful within a year. Or what? You'll receive five million dollars? You'll sue?

You and I both know there are no guarantees in life: For any number of reasons, you just may not find your mate anytime soon. One reason you may not find him is simply that you decide, after careful consideration, that you would rather live alone. For you, the costs of permanent companionship outweigh the rewards.

THE BENEFITS OF BEING SINGLE

Research on widowhood, published in 1973 by Helena Z. Lopata, indicated that the majority of the 254 unremarried widows in the study, all fifty years old or older, did not wish to remarry, even when they agreed that their husbands had been unusually good men. Similarly, many of the widows I interviewed were hesitant about remarriage, particularly when they had nursed a husband through a long final illness. A not unusual sentiment, perhaps a rationalization, expressed by older single women, widowed or divorced, is "I wouldn't want to end up as a nurse to a sick old man."

Such a seemingly harsh statement is often made in the abstract, when a woman isn't actually seeing someone. On the other hand, one charming widow whose husband had been confined to a wheelchair for ten years before his death, unable to walk or even to stand, says, "I looked after `Paul' the best I could for all those years, and I wouldn't hesitate to do it again for someone I love."

Although she does have an attentive lover who lives nearby, she, too, states firmly that she would not marry him, even though he proposes to her every Saturday night! Why not? Not because she fears being a caregiver to an invalid once more. Rather, she relishes the freedom from the more general domestic responsibilities that marriage would undoubtedly bring. "As things are, he takes care of his own laundry, his grocery shopping . . . and if I cook dinner, he brings wine and flowers. I like it this way. He lives close enough so I can see him whenever I want to, but I can also be independent."

Cynthia S. Smith's *Why Women Shouldn't Marry* expands on the theme of independence. The only reasons for a woman to marry are support and sperm, she writes. Why give up your freedom if you want or need neither? Smith's view is that women make far more sacrifices than men when they marry and that widows, especially, should consider alternatives. "You've been through enough!" she declares.

Smith's insistence that women give more to a marriage than men and get less from it is supported by the work of sociologist Jessie Bernard. In her book *The Future of Marriage*, Bernard claims that every marriage consists of two marriages—his and hers—and that his is better! Married men, her studies show, live longer than unmarried men; married men are healthier than unmarried men or married women; married men express more satisfaction with their lives than do unmarried men or married women. In fact, the only group expressing more satisfaction with their lives than married men is unmarried women.

More recent study of the figures reported in April 1995 adds further support to Bernard's findings. Linda Waite, president of the Population Association of America, also finds that, although the wedded state appears to be good for both sexes, women get less out of marriage than do men, and their level of sexual satisfaction does not usually rise after marriage. Married men, however, have sex twice as often as single men, and their level of satisfaction is higher than that of single men.

These general facts do not, of course, argue that marriage can never be an ideal arrangement for many women as well as for men. My own marriage allowed and encouraged substantial personal growth for both my husband and myself. I don't think either of us could have made the progress we did without the other. We were, however, teenagers when we met. We grew up together and learned over the years to tolerate each other's funny little ways and to ignore those behaviors that would have driven us crazy had we let them!

SUPPORT AND SPERM: DO YOU NEED THEM?

Until relatively recently, couples who fell in love expected—and were expected—to marry. Not many women in any society earned as much as men, and few could support themselves. If women did not marry, their usual option was to remain under their parents' roof, dependent children forever.

Falling in love, which many social scientists tell us is a social or cultural invention, provided the reason for a man and a woman to bind themselves together legally and set up a home for themselves and, before long, for their children. A woman exchanged dependency on her parents for dependency on her husband.

Nowadays, although most women still earn less than men do, they need not be married to leave their parents' homes. They do not depend on their parents for support. Further, financially independent women no longer have to stay in bad or unsatisfying marriages—which may account, at least in part, for some of the recent increase in late-life divorces.

Older people, retired or working, are even less likely than youngsters to need marriage for financial security. Indeed, marriage may prove financially detrimental. In her article "Love and Money" in the May-June 1995 issue of *Modern Maturity*, Linda Stern writes that couples who remain unmarried are spared an Internal Revenue Service "marriage penalty," which can be substantial. A widow's pension is sometimes lost if the woman remarries, as are workers' compensation benefits payable to a widow whose husband died in a work-related event. Social security benefits, too, may be reduced or lost. People considering remarriage should check carefully to determine possible losses or reductions of these kinds. Couples living together without marriage should also be sure that estate plans are clearly written to avoid possible disagreements with more traditional heirs.

True, two incomes are bigger than one, and a couple, married and with both working, may be able to afford more spacious living accommodations and more material objects than a man and a woman living separately. However, this reason alone may not be enough to lead a couple to marry today.

The need to have children, the only other reason besides support that Smith considers compelling enough for a woman to marry, is probably not an issue for most couples past fifty, despite the latest advances in reproductive medicine that allow women to give birth later and later in their lives!

THE JOYS OF INDEPENDENCE

Even some women who felt they wanted nothing more than to remarry after the death of a husband or after a divorce, find the urgency of this desire waning with time. Women may begin to appreciate the control they have over their time and money. Those who have never lived alone before are able, perhaps for the first time in their lives, to come and go as they please without telling daddy or hubby where they are going, with whom, and when they will be back. They can take themselves to the movies in the afternoon without having to explain their movements to anyone, without feeling guilty for being cooped up indoors when the sun is shining. They can see the movies they prefer, tune in to the television programs they enjoy, rather than giving in to others' tastes and wishes. A woman may never have to watch, or listen to, football again unless, of course, she wants to.

Independence can be heady stuff. Assuming a woman is keeping track of her income and expenditures, she may decide to buy that lovely but expensive outfit in the department store window, again without consulting her spouse, without waiting for his approval, or without his obvious disapproval when she carries her purchases home.

Seline's Story

"Seline," who had been a widow for over four years after a long and good marriage, was one of those women who thought she wanted nothing other than remarriage—to a man similar in temperament to her husband, if she could find him. In two years, she had met and dated several decent men, but none quite fit the bill. "Harry," a widower, a decent man of similar cultural background to her own and to her late husband's, was the first man she considered seriously as a potential mate.

For several months Harry had been courting her patiently, ardently, and caringly. He sensed her reluctance to settle down with him, even though she was, as yet, not aware of it herself. She liked his company, enjoyed his gentle sense of humor, yet she found a day with him too long and a weekend *much* too long. She was relieved when he left, glad to have her house to herself again.

"I don't know what's the matter with me," she confided in me. "I feel so guilty. As though I'm leading him on. He's a good man; I like him very much but . . ."

Together, we probed her feelings. As Harry traveled some distance to be with Seline, she allowed him to stay overnight at her house, not in her bed, she said, but in the spare room. He agreed to this arrangement although he was disappointed not to be sleeping with her. "I don't feel ready for that, yet" she said. "It would indicate a commitment that I'm not sure I can make. And you know the way we were brought up; we don't go to bed with people we aren't really sure about!"

Early in the morning after his first stopover, Harry woke her with a cup of tea, first rapping on the bedroom door to announce himself. "I know he meant well. He was trying to show me what a splendidly domestic creature he is, but I was *really* annoyed. I spent much of the day asking myself why I felt that way. After all, I often make myself an early morning cup of tea and take it back to bed with me."

Her irritation, she concluded, was at being pulled out of a deep sleep, sleep that she felt she needed. She is normally an early riser, and her days are filled with strenuous activities; that morning, she happened to sleep a little longer than usual. "I know this sounds unreasonable, but how dare someone take it on himself to wake me up?"

Seline's feelings may, indeed, seem unreasonable and her guilt about "the poor man (how can I expect him to read my mind?)" reflects that. Her annoyance with Harry over this small matter and other similarly trivial intrusions ("He picked up my crossword while I was pouring him a second cup of coffee and filled in one of the clues. It made me really angry, though I know it shouldn't have.") shows that she has become used to living alone. Not only has she developed her own routines as a single person, she *likes* them and resents their being ignored, even though "the poor man" can't be expected to know them unless he is told.

"It seems so unfair to expect him to fit in with *my* ways, but I like the life I've made for myself. True, I fret over the chores and all the responsibility that used to be shared, but I'm proud of the way I manage. I'm not sure I want someone telling me 'better' ways to do things."

Seline has not yet resolved the situation with Harry but has become aware, at least, of her own uncertainty and will not rush into a marriage or other shared domestic arrangement. She is, as she says, "still evolving" as an independent human being. If Harry cares enough for her, he will continue to be patient.

Many older single men, both divorced men and widowers, just as women who have learned to enjoy single life, prefer not to remarry, although this may not be what they say—or what they want you to believe! A man who has lived on his own for ten or fifteen years—all the while declaring how much he wants to find the right woman to marry—is most unlikely ever to relinquish his single state.

In the early years after his wife's death or his divorce, he may have been helpless in the kitchen and hopeless with the laundry. As time passed, he learned to cook for himself—and he cooks what *he* likes the way *he* likes it! He, like his female counterpart, may have found some advantages in living alone and being accountable to no one. Used to discussing a potential purchase at length with his wife—say a new set of golf clubs or some state-of-the-art video equipment—and often being dissuaded from such an extravagance, he may now indulge himself in ways never before possible and may not want to give up that prerogative.

Many women, then, and men may conclude that living alone, while it may not be perfect and is sometimes lonely, is preferable to making the sacrifices necessary to sharing hearth and home with someone else.

WHAT TODAY'S NEW WOMAN CAN TEACH US

On a recent camping trip with the Sierra Club, I met a group of women in their mid-forties to mid-fifties whose conversation stopped me in my tracks. They made me realize that some ways of thinking about the place of men in our lives may not only be out of date but may also stop us from reaching our own potential; they may be cutting us off from joys we didn't know we could experience.

Many of us grew up during a time when women who did not marry were pitied as spinsters. They were viewed, and viewed themselves, as undesirable and incomplete. A single woman was labeled an old maid as early as in her late twenties. Some of us still hold this view, leading to many an interesting discussion with our daughters, who don't seem to be in any hurry to marry and give us grandchildren!

Our daughters in their twenties and thirties, like those women I met climbing in the Sierras, have come of age since the women's liberation movement of the 1970s and hold their own view of how men fit into their lives. Our daughters, most of them, do want children—later on, perhaps—and would like to rear those children in a family with two parents.

However, the somewhat older women I met on this camping trip—educated women with careers—are no longer "one man away from poverty." Nor, given their age, do they need men to father their children. They enjoy men's company, but they have learned that they don't have to live *with* them to live.

It may be a lesson we can learn to our advantage and that men, particularly some older men, may have to learn, as one man's story may show.

Jeb's Story

"Jeb," at sixty, had been married for decades and had fathered three daughters, all now grown and independent, when his wife broke it to him that she really preferred women, and she was off to live with one. You can imagine what this did to the poor fellow's sense of self, of masculinity, even if the marriage "hadn't been good" for some time. Jeb, a biologist, took himself to the Third World for a couple of years with the Peace Corps to think things through and plan how to live the rest of his life.

Back in the United States, he rented an apartment month to month and set himself three goals: to find a woman to share his life; to move to a rural or semirural area, either in America or abroad; and to find some useful, satisfying work in his field. He gave himself eight months to accomplish all of this.

"Perhaps you should move first," I suggested, "and find a woman who is already where you think you want to live."

"Well, I've been round and round on this, and I've decided to find the woman first as there may be less selection in the place I might want to settle."

He placed a personal advertisement in his large city's newspaper: "DM. 62, well-educ, travld, fin sec, fit. ISO [in search of] romance, adventure, caring, sharing, LTR [long-term relationship]."

A few weeks after he advertised, I asked him how the search was going.

"I've given it up," he said, tersely.

"But why? What happened? How many women did you meet?"

"About a dozen. But they're all the same."

"The same? What do you mean?"

"Well, they're all intelligent, nice-looking, professionals with houses and careers and . . ."

"You mean they have *lives*?" I interrupted.

"Yes. And I can't believe how unadventurous they are. They have their *routines*, and they expect me to just *slot into* their calendars. They aren't willing to even consider starting a new life."

"Why would they? With someone they don't even know. It takes time to make a decision like that."

"Why? It doesn't take me any time. *I know* what I want."

"But you don't have anything to give up. No home, no job. Your family is scattered. You're as free as the air. These women have worked hard to establish themselves; why would they sacrifice that?"

"What sacrifice? What's a *house*? Things? I'm talking about building an exciting new life with someone."

Here was an educated man, yes, of pleasant enough appearance, but otherwise an unknown quantity, expecting one advertisement in the newspaper to bring him a wonderful woman. This woman would be willing to give up her hard-won security to walk off into the sunset with him, hand in hand, without his making any effort to woo, to please, to win her, without his taking the time to know what *she* might be seeking. He didn't understand that grown-up women today have all kinds of options and that the men who want to be with them may, indeed, have to "slot into" their lives—if, indeed, they have a place at all.

Sandra's Story

"Sandra," one of the women in the camping group, has just sold the business she had established five years before, and the gain from the sale will support her for several years. She is weighing her choices. In her early fifties, she is fit, active, attractive, intelligent, self-sufficient, funny—and she feels she can do anything she wants.

"The whole world is waiting for me," she says.

She might live in Tuscany for a year, study art in Paris, purchase a round-the-world airline ticket. A man in her life? Yes, there is someone she cares for; but she has been married and divorced three times, she will not have any more children, and she does not need financial support. She is free to set out on adventures that she could not consider earlier in her life.

Will her man accompany Sandra on her travels? She's not sure. She is fond of him but . . . "This is a most marvelous time for women in our situation," she almost sings the words. "We've built a circle of friends and family, and leaving them to explore some other style of life means we widen that circle still more. We add new friends, discover new ways of being. We are truly privileged."

Agreed. Still, not every woman will be able, or want, to leave her familiar life. However, neither need she wait for a man to come along, scoop her up, and "take her away from all this." Women are changing direction, seeking their own adventures, making decisions that may not include men at all.

WHEN LOVE DOESN'T EQUAL MARRIAGE OR LIVE-IN COMPANIONSHIP

Finding meaning in life—a reason to start each day—is a serious pursuit for all human beings, young and old. It becomes especially important when much of what used to define us has been lost or put aside. The answer to "What do you do?" tells others who we are. It also confirms and reconfirms our identity for ourselves. "I'm a housewife"—even "I'm *only* a housewife," the slightly apologetic reply given by some women since the feminist movement encouraged women into offices and factories—reassures us that we have a place to be and a job to do.

In the later years, retirement, though it may be anticipated with pleasure, strips us of one of the more important aspects of our selves, our status in the professional or working world. The housewife, too, even though she does not retire, no longer has youngsters to care for. The widowed or divorced housewife cooks and cleans only for herself.

THE MANY FACES OF LOVE

The challenge is to reinvent ourselves, to find new identities, new ways of loving and being loved that may, or may not, include romantic or sexual love, and new reasons to anticipate each day with pleasure. It may mean inventing, or becoming part of, a new "family," finding ways to be among children, or it may mean inventing a new *self*—perhaps finally *becoming* the artist or the writer we've always day-dreamed about being, now that we are free of responsibilities towards others.

Finding a New "Family"

The woman with grandchildren who live nearby and whom she sees frequently is likely to have a sense of continuity with the past, reasons to plan ahead, and a proud and legitimate new role as grandma that helps sustain her sense of self and an honorable place within a family.

The current trend towards deferred parenting, especially among career-oriented couples, leaves many people without grandchildren at an age when *their* parents had grandchildren already in high school or college. My own father, for instance, was forty-four years old when his first grandson was born. Now, some men are waiting until their forties to *start* their families, and their wives are in their late thirties, even early forties, when the first child is born.

The grandparent role, then, the role most of us expected to play, may not be ours until we are quite old, if ever. And even those who *are* grandparents may live thousands of miles away from their grandchildren and seldom see them.

Surrogate Grandparenting

For those who really miss children in their lives, who get dewy-eyed at the sight of a new baby, who long to hold a child or romp with children in the park or on the living room floor, who enjoy nothing as much as watching the changes in a child's face as he listens to a tale unfolding, the way to fill that need may be to become someone's surrogate grandparent.

Those same children who are born late in their parents' lives—that current trend again—sometimes, because of their parents' ages, come into a two-generation family and don't have any grandparents. My own research (described in my book *Last Chance Children*) has shown that such youngsters feel happier as children when they have older people around them who care about them and who "stand in" as grandparents, especially when their parents are busy professionals, as is often the case these days.

Here would seem a perfect matching of needs. Look around you in your neighborhood. Perhaps you already know some busy parents. Talk to them, and you may find they would love to have a nearby "grandparent" for their children. Even if their own parents are still living, they may live far away, so your wisdom and experience may be appreciated in all kinds of ways. With luck, and after establishing mutual trust with the parents, your ready-made family is close at hand.

Other ways of participating in the lives of children, if this is what you most miss in your life, may be to give some of your time to your local kindergarten or grade school. Small children love to listen to stories and to have books read to them. However, many parents, because of the demands of their jobs or careers, no longer have time for this enjoyable activity. Schools encourage—and need—the participation of people in the community as teachers' aids.

Youngsters in the hospital, too, sick babies and small children, may need someone to sit with them and talk or gently croon, or to hold them and rock them. People who regularly help in this way tell me the satisfaction and love they receive far outweigh the "sacrifice" of their time.

FINDING AND FALLING IN LOVE WITH YOUR OWN CREATIVE SELF

Many of us in our fifties, sixties, seventies, and older grew up believing in the rightness of loving companionship. If we were married, or knew the joy of partnership, of sharing life's pleasures and problems, we have a hard time imagining real happiness on our own. We have a hard time giving up the idea that we need someone else to complete us, even if our partnerships were far from ideal, even if our marriages ended in divorce. Old ways of thought and old habits die hard.

Now, though, women, young as well as old, have given themselves permission to enjoy being single, to be "selfish," and to live for themselves. Alternatives to marriage or a long-term relationship include the joy that comes from finding and developing your creative talent.

For most of your life, you have lived through and for others and have been able to give only spare time to your own interests. Spare time, when you are rearing a family, is scarce indeed. The woman in a nine-to-five job followed by weekends of shopping and household, garden, automotive, and book-keeping chores must put aside personal fulfillment for the sake of the children.

Now may be your time, at last, this "most marvelous time for women in our situation." And if not now, when?

Ask yourself the following question, and without thinking about it for too long, write down at least five answers:

If you could to do anything in the world, regardless of anyone else's opinion, what would you choose to do?

What have you written? Are there any surprises? Didn't you always know in your heart that you wanted to:

§ Go back to school and earn a degree?

§ Skydive?

§ Paint glorious daubs on huge canvasses?

§ Design and build furniture?

§ Understand computers?

§ Write a novel?

§ Walk across the United States?

§ Run an English tea shop?

§ Give marvelous parties?

§ Know how to blow glass?

§ Examine desert flowers?

§ Tell fortunes?

§ Climb mountains?

§ Speak Chinese?

§ Play the bassoon?

§ Spend a year in Italy?

At first blush, some of your answers will seem wild and totally out of the question. Why? Everything on the list above is attainable—for someone who wants it enough to begin planning. At least *some* of the items on your list can be realized. Indulge yourself! Think only of what *you* want right now and what would please you *most*. Put aside your feelings of guilt; forget "what people would say"; stop thinking of how the money you would spend, whether much or little, could be used for some more "worthy" purpose; sift the possible from the unlikely and begin to think of yourself not as who you *are*, complete and shaped by the life you have led, but as a "work in progress."

No matter what your age, assuming reasonably good health, it is not too late to change direction. Just as when you launched yourself back into dating, you'll need courage to discover yourself and value yourself enough to do what you really want. You'll need to prepare and plan. This may be the most challenging and the most rewarding effort you will ever make.

Albert's Story

"Albert," a fellow student during my undergraduate years, had just turned eighty-two when we marched together to receive our bachelor's degrees. We were all proud that day, but none stood up more straight or smiled more broadly when presented with his diploma than this ever-young, elderly man. As a young person, he'd had to help support his brothers and sisters; later, he was responsible for his own family of sons and daughters. Always bright and inquisitive, he read as much as he could, bringing home bags of books from the library; he couldn't afford to buy many books of his own.

His interests were wide: literature, history, archeology, anthropology. There was hardly a subject he hadn't read about. Even after his children had left home, his responsibilities continued to be heavy. Abigail, his wife of many years, became disabled. Added to his hours at the plant every day were all the household chores and the care of his wife.

Only after he retired from his job on a modest pension did he allow his old dream of attaining a college degree to become a possibility. He talked about it, hesitantly at first, with Abigail. She encouraged him to explore the local colleges, both the state and the community college. Then, though, Abigail's health declined so sharply that she needed constant care. Albert put his dream aside once more, nursing his wife for several years before she died.

When I first met him, he had completed the first two years of college work and was highly respected on the campus. His participation in the classroom was eager, but he was wise enough not to take over the discussion, even though he had far more experience of the world and had read more than most of the other students.

Albert loved being a college student. He was on campus every day, studying in the library, experimenting in the chemistry lab, meeting with faculty members, eating his packed lunch in the quad, usually with a group of young people who might have been his grandchildren, or even his great-grandchildren, but were, in this setting, his contemporaries.

At the commencement ceremony, the president of the college presented Albert with a special silk stole to wear over his graduation gown; the entire assembly stood and applauded—and whistled and hollered and shrieked!

Albert did not need a college degree to progress in the world of work. His need was to fulfil himself. He was exceptional in realizing his dream so late in life, but he was not the only mature student on campus, even at that time.

Now, more and more people are returning to college in their fifties, sixties, and later to earn degrees and, yes, to start new careers—often the kinds of careers that once would have been considered an indulgence or simply an impossibility. Newspapers and magazines like *Modern Maturity* often run stories about these enterprising men and women.

In the past, few women, for instance, could aspire to law degrees. Now, since age is no barrier to practicing law, some older people are studying for, and passing, the bar, hanging out their own shingles and taking cases that interest them. Others become social workers or counselors, often specializing in concerns of older people. With an aging population, this is a growing field. Still others are able to build small businesses simply by doing what they most enjoy.

Madge's Story

"Madge" had stayed in an unhappy marriage for thirty years until her last child was launched and independent. Then she sued for divorce.

She surprised her friends and family by beginning work at an animal shelter, at first earning little more than minimum wage. As she learned more about the laws and ordinances that apply to animals, as she became more knowledgeable about the care and feeding and breeding of animals, she became more valuable to her employers. Finally, Madge established her own business.

Madge doesn't make a fortune, but she is happier than she has ever been in her life. She regularly walks dogs for busy professionals, she is expanding her kennels, and she has recently begun breeding Irish wolfhounds—dogs she has always loved. She is now, moreover, so knowledgeable about wolfhounds that she is often called to serve as a consultant to groups devoted to that breed.

Madge, once she "freed" herself of her job as an "ordinary" housewife and mother, changed her life completely, finding real joy doing what she wants to do.

Olivia's Story

"Olivia," married in her late twenties, lived a conventional and contented life. She prepared baked goods for the PTA; went door to door with her daughters as they sold Girl Scout cookies; knitted sweaters of her own design for her family; and watched a lot of television as she waited for her girls to come home from their dates. After her daughters married and left the area, she found an office job in her daughters' old school and held it until she reached retirement age. Only weeks into her retirement, her husband died, leaving her financially comfortable but with nothing much to live for.

After months of mourning—and hours on the telephone with her daughters on the other side of the country—she signed up for an art class at the local community college. She knew she had to do something to fill her days, and she had always had a good eye for line and color.

Her instructor saw immediately that Olivia had a natural, "primitive" talent. She was disappointed that he gave her only the most basic guidance, but he told her he was afraid of spoiling her style by shaping her work in any way. He encouraged her to simply express herself on the canvas without regard to artistic traditions or trends.

Within two years, Olivia had produced dozens of marvelous, vibrant paintings, some huge, some as tiny as postcards. When I met her, a studio addition to her house, with enormous windows capturing the northern light, was just being completed, and she was negotiating with a major gallery for a showing of several of her paintings. She told me she felt more fulfilled, more truly happy, than at any time in her life.

"I had no idea that I could be, that I was, a real artist. People always enjoyed the little pictures I drew on letters and on birthday cards, but to discover that I can create something seriously beautiful . . . it's a real joy."

Your Story?

What about you? You know you have at least one novel simmering in your brain. You've always had a hankering to get it on paper. Why aren't you writing it? It's too late? You are too old? Nonsense! Know that the highly acclaimed *Jules and Jim* was written as a first novel by a man in his seventies.

It'll take too long? You'll never get it finished? If you type one page a day into your word processor or onto your typewriter, you'll complete the novel in less than a year. And if you don't turn out those pages, what will you have at the end of that time? Only your unfulfilled longing.

You aren't sure how to start? Bookstores and libraries have shelves of books on planning and structuring a novel. Classes in creative writing abound.

You *can* invent a new identity. You *can* be a writer or a painter or a mountain climber, or whatever it is your dream to be. You can be complete and self-sufficient. The love you have been looking for may be hidden within you.

"The Whole World Is Waiting for Me"

D o you remember those words—"The whole world is waiting for me"—said by Sandra, of the Sierra Club camping
trip? My hope, now that you have read through this book,
is that you too can make the same joyous statement.

The world *is* waiting for you! All you need is the courage to
go out and meet it. Paul Newman, speaking of what he has
learned about directing movies, says his main task is to find out
what gives the actors confidence "because it liberates them to do
things they wouldn't otherwise do."

My task, too, has been to encourage you to build confidence
in yourself; to help you to know who you are and what you really want; and to suggest many different ways you might look for
love and fulfillment. Those ways may be things you wouldn't
otherwise do but that might have rewards you could not have
imagined.

PLEASE LET ME HEAR FROM YOU

Almost every day, someone tells me how she met the man in
her life, or how a friend or a sister or a cousin found her husband or companion. I love these stories! They constantly affirm

that people in later life are looking for and finding affection, romance, and contentment.

Just yesterday, my neighbor told me about her friend, "Laura," a widow nearing seventy, who has recently married a man some nine years younger than she, and who is as happy as any new bride could be. After she was widowed, Laura found that her income would barely cover the upkeep of her house. She hated the thought of moving, so she advertised a large room and bath for rent. The first renter to come and go was a young fellow in his twenties, but the second man came—and never left. Laura married him.

Here is a case of a knight who actually *did* ride up to the house—although not on a white charger—and carry off the fair lady! It shows that almost anything can happen, once you take steps to *make* it happen.

And this morning I heard from an old friend in the Midwest who arranged a "bring a friend" party. Each of the women brought a single man in the right age group, a man with whom she is *not* romantically involved—an office mate, or someone from the church, or a family member, or some other suitable, unattached person. My friend reports that some fascinating mixing and matching took place!

Love comes in many forms and is found in many places.

The direct resources—personal advertisements, online services, singles events, dances and mixers, dating services or matchmakers—are all straightforward methods of meeting members of the opposite sex.

The indirect resources—a wide range of activities that interest you—are ways of enriching your life and of making new friends among men and women who share your passions. Being out in the community brings you into circles of acquaintances that you would not otherwise have met and where you may find romance.

Finally, discovering your own creativity, developing your own skills and talents, can bring you rewards you never dreamed of.

Please let me know *your* story. Which methods work for you? Tell me about your adventures. You can write to me,

Monica B. Morris, in care of Avery Publishing Group, 120 Old Broadway, Garden City Park, New York 11040. I'll be waiting for your letters.

Meanwhile, whatever the route you choose, I wish you love.

Index